Deep River Crossings

Deep River Crossings

Lorrie C. Reed

RESOURCE *Publications* • Eugene, Oregon

DEEP RIVER CROSSINGS

Resource Publications
An Imprint of Wipf and Stock Publishers
199 W. 8th Ave., Suite 3
Eugene, OR 97401

www.wipfandstock.com

PAPERBACK ISBN: 979-8-3852-2480-7
HARDCOVER ISBN: 979-8-3852-2481-4
EBOOK ISBN: 979-8-3852-2482-1

VERSION NUMBER 06/25/24

Contents

Abbreviations

ADA	Americans with Disabilities Act
ASCAP	American Society of Composers and Publishers
BLM	Black Lives Matter
CAPS	Community Alternative Policing Strategy
CPE	Clinical Pastoral Education
CT	Computed Tomography
ED	Emergency Department
EMT	Emergency Medical Technician
HGTV	Home and Gardening TV
ICU	Intensive Care Unit
IV	Intravenous
NFL	National Football League
NICU	Neonatal Intensive Care Unit
PEDS	Pediatrics
PRN	pro re nata, when necessary
STAT	Medical abbreviation meaning "immediately" in Latin
TBI	Traumatic Brain Injury
TLC	Tender Loving Care

Prologue: 2001

The first-year college students in Hannah's 8 a.m. applied statistics class were a mix of tired and eager faces. Some still felt the effects of a late night, with droopy eyes and yawning mouths, while others appeared more alert and engaged. Despite their varying levels of wakefulness, all students seemed genuinely interested as she explained the nature of the error term in regression equations.

"The outcome of a regression equation is equal to the weighted sum of its known variables plus an error term, something the known variables or their interactions cannot explain. It is the error term that balances the equation in the end. This suggests that the whole is always greater than the sum of its identifiable parts."

She assigned the students to groups to explore this concept further, encouraging them to draw parallels from their experiences. Upon reconvening, a vibrant brainstorming session unfolded.

"What are examples of the error term?" Hannah prompted them and wrote their responses on the whiteboard.

"It seems like an unseen force that binds everything together," one student proposed.

"Any other thoughts?" she probed.

"To me, the error term bridges contradictions and uncertainties."

"It acts like a spiritual essence. Like Ashe, the life force that guides us on this journey."

"The error term is like the truth that contradicts all lies."

"The error term might just be time or eternity."

"Is it like synergy?"

"I think it transcends the hope found in Pandora's box."

Occasionally, a stifled yawn or a furtive glance at the clock betrayed some students' fatigue, but overall, they showed enthusiasm for the subject.

"Great ideas! We'll look at the question deeper after the break," she informed them, signaling a fifteen-minute recess and instructing them to reconvene at 9:05.

She was unaware that, as the students regathered, a monumental event was unfolding. Flight 175 was crashing into the South Tower of the World Trade Center. This cataclysmic event disrupted the world's rhythm, obliterating everyone's notions of safety and security. A palpable sense of disequilibrium pervaded as the symbolic equation of life seemed to have lost its stability.

The event on September 11, 2001, at 9:30 a.m., thrust Hannah into a vortex of unease and disorientation. The insights she once held dear suddenly appeared obsolete. From then on, she struggled to regain a new sense of steadiness, a quest that led her away from academics into ministry and beyond.

1

2010 **Return to Town**

Hannah couldn't help but feel excitement as she took in the sights. The Bowie family was headed to their new home, north of Jordan Avenue near the Grandview River in Lewis Town, where Hannah had grown up. She looked forward to getting reacquainted with the community; many changes had occurred since she left. Hannah recalled Lewis Town's rich history. It was founded in the 1920s, with Jordan Avenue dividing the community along racial and economic lines. North of Jordan, toward the river, grand Victorian mansions lined the streets, their reddish brick houses adorned with bright green and warm brown awnings. The yards were a sight to behold—flowering annuals of all colors and rich, perennial greenery formed collars around the walkways and borders. The shops, civic buildings, movie theaters, and library were all there. Riverside Park was on the north side. Mostly, the residents were White, although many Black professionals, schoolteachers, and shop owners lived there, too. None of Hannah's blood relatives owned houses north of Jordan before Urban Renewal.

South of Jordan was where Hannah grew up in an economically depressed neighborhood, about one hundred square blocks, a curious blending of rural squalor and suburban promise. Even though Lewis Town was considered a suburb back then, many south-side residents kept animals. Her aunt and uncle had a hound dog, chickens, a rooster, and a goat. In their part of town, cyclone fences separated the yards from each other. In those days, many homeowners still had outhouses. The government eventually demolished the squalid homes to pave the way for affordable public housing designated for qualifying families. With the aid of Community Development Block Grants, the town had recently started constructing new housing, parkland, and commercial businesses along the riverfront. After much soul-searching and studying in the seminary, Hannah had accepted a job as a chaplain at the new hospital on the southwest side of town, just a short distance from her childhood residence. Hannah almost gave herself whiplash, trying to see the changes that had taken place in Lewis Town since she left more than twenty years ago. Reflecting on her childhood, Hannah realized how far she had come.

She recalled the first house she and Phillip had bought when their kids were young. After living in apartments for many years, Hannah told Phillip it was time for them to buy a house. Phillip said it couldn't be done. Hannah, on the other hand, said, "Watch me!" They saved money and moved into their first house when the children were in grammar school. As their careers advanced, they purchased other houses. Today was special because Hannah was coming home to the town where she had grown up. Her quest to reach the river north of Jordan Avenue was finally a reality. Hannah looked forward to settling in their new home where she could reflect on the nearby river's beauty on her enclosed back deck.

###

Hannah couldn't help but chuckle to herself. Here, she was still searching for her purpose in life. Acting out her desire to serve others, she had frequently changed careers, testing the deep, turbulent waters in education, academia, research, and chaplaincy. On a whim, she applied for this hospital chaplain job at the Southwest Medical Center. When the manager told her he wanted to hire her, she felt a prayer was answered. Although she still had a CPE unit to complete before being eligible for Board certification, this job allowed her to test her wings in a level-one trauma center.

Southwest Medical Center was a 350-bed facility providing patient care in various medical specialties. Its Emergency Department was state-of-the-art, serving up to thirty patients at a time. Equipped with the most up-to-date technology, each bay stood ready to encounter whatever came through the doors of the ED. The hospital had multiple operating rooms, an intensive care unit, and a neonatal intensive care unit. Patients received top-notch care from a team of doctors, nurses, and other healthcare professionals. The trauma center presented a fast-paced and challenging work environment.

When Hannah arrived at 6:50 a.m., the Spiritual Care office was dark except for the overhead light that was always on. After filling her water bottle, she clocked in and returned to check the list of triggers for the day. As she began her rounds, Hannah walked down the corridor, sidestepping medical equipment and nursing personnel.

"Happy Friday," the unit clerk greeted her as she exited the elevator.

"Did you bring all this sunshine?" Hannah smiled in response.

"No, but I appreciate it. Honestly, the weather is unpredictable this time of year," the clerk quipped.

"You're right. It could be worse. Have a good one." Hannah replied.

Hannah started with the patient in room 223, who needed a healthcare power of attorney.

"Good morning. I'm Hannah, one of the chaplains. How's it going today?"

"I can't complain," the patient said, shoving the remains of her scrambled eggs around her plate. She had not touched her toast.

"I stopped by to see if you were ready to complete your healthcare power of attorney."

"No. I'm tired today. Why don't you come back tomorrow."

"No problem. I'll put you down for a return visit."

Undaunted, Hannah continued her rounds, making small talk and completing forms.

###

Hannah's children, Calvin and Denise, were new to Lewis Town High School. The Lewis Town High School was notorious for its culture of cliques and gangs. Hannah was worried because Calvin and Denise found it hard to fit in at their last few schools. Calvin often grew impatient when he was bored. Academically gifted and intellectually curious, Calvin excelled in school, consistently earning top marks and a spot on the honor roll. Music, however, was where his heart was at peace. He played the trombone in his last school's marching band with disciplined precision and was often absorbed in playing the piano, mastering tunes by ear with a near-magical skill.

Denise possessed a rare blend of curiosity, foresight, and creativity. Her dancing was a beacon of light in a world filled with darkness, a reminder that we all have the potential to soar to new heights if we believe in ourselves and our ability to overcome. For Denise, dance was a powerful metaphor for self-discovery and empowerment, a reminder that beauty and strength can emerge from even the darkest circumstances. In telling her story through dance, Denise found a way to exhibit beauty, strength, and hope.

Determined to help her children acclimate to the new environment, Hannah contacted her old friend Indigo, whom she had known since the seventh grade. The friends had stayed in touch through social media. Indigo taught in the math program at the high school and also served as the sponsor of the school's fine arts program. Hannah arranged for Calvin and Denise to enroll in the after-school music and dance programs, both of which had an outstanding reputation. Entering Indigo's classroom brought back old memories. Colorful objects met the eye at every turn. The air was a mix of the smell of new construction paper and old chalk dust. An expansive chalkboard dominated the south wall, while charts on the north wall revealed secrets to calculating means, medians, and modes. Indigo was delighted to accept Hannah's children into the school's enrichment activities. Denise signed up for dance, and Calvin opted for the band.

The school's pep band performed at the Friday night football games. As a band booster, Hannah attended the games and did her part to unite the still-divided Lewis Town community. Grudges among the town's factions had endured for generations. Given the continuing animosity, reconciliation was not likely to occur soon. As Hannah looked into the bleachers for the home team, she could easily detect the divisions among the spectators, who had formed enclaves based on community loyalty. There was a significant police presence at the concession stand.

Later that year, Calvin participated in the Lewis Town Neighborhood Association Memorial Day parade. The parade was like no other, with everyone invited to participate and no one sitting on the sidelines watching. Participants from all walks of life stepped along the route, sporting their streamers, noisemakers, and confetti. Families pulled wagons with small children screaming with excitement. The drum and bugle corps marched behind high-stepping majorettes. Calvin proudly played his trombone as the brass section strutted down the street in colorful outfits. Northside businesses drove cars decorated with placards to advertise their commerce. Politicians carried campaign signs and shook hands with neighborhood residents who joined the procession along the route. The parade route ended in Riverfront Park, where Hannah had been forbidden to go as a child. Many local vendors distributed discount coupons and advertisements for introductory offers. Local restaurants had set up food booths to sell sample portions of their dishes. Artists, crafters, and musicians were present, along with predators who waited for opportunities to pounce on unsuspecting residents.

Denise had honed her skills well enough by the spring term to perform at the spring recital. She performed a jazz dance to "Black Butterfly." With her body undulating and her arms fluttering, she gracefully reenacted the journey of a chrysalis transitioning from cocoon to maturation, eventually being transformed into a stunning butterfly. Tears rolled down Hannah's cheeks as she watched her daughter perform. The dance touched Hannah on many levels. It spoke of Hannah's struggles at the intersection of race, class, and gender and brought to mind the travails of that great cloud of Black female witnesses who had preceded her from the beginning of time. As an undeniable statement of change, the song expressed disappointment while simultaneously promising hope. Indeed, while everyone had been sleeping, the promises of freedom and equality had not been kept.

In addition to dance, Denise spent her weekends visiting hospice patients and reading to them. Her warm smile and kind heart brought comfort to patients who were struggling with illness and loneliness. She brought light into the lives of those she touched, and her presence was like a ray of sunshine in the otherwise sterile and sometimes bleak hospice environment. One day, Denise met a former English teacher who was undergoing cancer treatment. Seeing the teacher in such a vulnerable state was heartbreaking for Denise, but she was determined to bring some joy and comfort during the teacher's time of need. Denise spent hours talking to her and listening to stories about her experiences from the good old times.

On her way back from the hospice center one day, Denise walked through Riverfront Park to clear her mind and relax after a long weekend of volunteering. Calvin was to meet up with her there to ensure she got home safely. Denise felt at peace as she strolled along the riverbank, feeling the sun's warmth on her face and the gentle breeze rustling through the trees. But her tranquility was soon shattered by the sound of harsh voices and mocking laughter behind her.

Turning around, Denise saw a group of people she recognized from school—students known for their bullying and cruel behavior. As they approached Denise with sneers on their faces and malice in their eyes, Denise felt a surge of fear and anger rise within her. She knew these were not people with her best interests at heart, and she braced herself for whatever they had in store.

"You don't belong here, outsider," one sneered, pointing toward the other end of town. "No matter how hard you try, you'll never fit in."

Denise felt her heart sink at their hurtful words, but she refused to let them see her weakness. She stood tall, chin held high, and looked them straight in the eye.

"I'm not afraid of you! I will not let your ignorance bring me down."

The bullies laughed at her defiance, their taunts growing louder and more vicious. They circled her, blocking her path and making her feel trapped. Denise's heart raced as she searched for a way out of the tense situation, but she knew she had to stand her ground. She couldn't let them intimidate her into silence.

Just as the tension heightened, a familiar voice cut through the chaos. "What's going on here?"

Denise turned to see Calvin standing a few feet away, his eyes blazing with anger and concern. When he heard the commotion, he rushed to see what was happening. The bullies faltered at the sight of someone their size who dared to stand up to them.

"This is none of your business," one spat, but Calvin refused to back down.

"Denise is my sister. And it is my business," Calvin said.

The bullies hesitated, unsure what to do in the face of Calvin's unwavering boldness. They exchanged uneasy glances, sensing they had crossed a line they shouldn't have. Slowly, they backed away, muttering insults as they retreated.

Denise released a shaky breath, relief flooding her as the tension dissipated. She turned to Calvin, tears welling up in her eyes. "I hate this place, Calvin. I'll be glad when we graduate and get out of here."

###

Hannah smiled at Phillip through the candlelight. It was rare for the couple to enjoy time off together. Mood music played softly in the background, mingling with the hum of conversation and subdued laughter. This weekend, Hannah and Phillip were celebrating their seventeenth wedding anniversary. Confident, strong, and determined, Phillip had a twinkle in his eye, and a warm smile lit up his face. Hannah remembered the day she met Phillip as a first-year student at the downstate university. She had just finished unpacking her clothes and tucking the last few items in the dresser drawers of her new dormitory room. It was getting close to dinner time, so she went to the dining hall for a bite. Newly arrived coeds packed the room. Decked out in Afros of various shapes and sizes and adorned with beaded shirts and bell bottoms, these college students greeted each other with peals of laughter and trash talk while the smell of French fries and the sounds of "Hot Fun in the Summertime" wafted through the air. A few people danced on the sidelines. Two or three card games were in progress. Onlookers cheered for their favorite teams as the Bid Whist players slammed cards on the table, hoping to run a Boston. The party was in full swing and did not seem to be winding down at any time soon when she spotted Phillip. He was sitting at a card table with a deck of cards in his hand. She asked him if he needed a partner. They have been together ever since.

After getting to know each other better, Hannah discovered they were from the Chicago metropolitan area. She was from Lewis Town, and he was from the south side of Chicago. He had come to the university to study engineering and computer science, and she had come to study literature. Both of them were glad to be away from home for the first time, where they could explore the world, discover its complexities, make their own mistakes, and live or die trying.

Their attraction to each other was instant. Over time, they grew to adore each other and discovered new things together. One afternoon, they wandered around campus on an excursion in search of their classroom buildings. They visited the bookstore to pick up the textbooks they would need for the semester. Later, they strolled through the campus woods and sat by the lake at dusk, discussing their schedules and the intensity of their course loads. Several days later, Hannah reported to her social studies lecture hall class. Even though the auditorium held around two hundred students, she spotted Phillip in the crowd. There was no mistaking his slender build and walnut complexion. When he saw her, he waved and pointed toward the empty seat next to him.

They fell in love quickly and got married after their sophomore year. In the early days of their marriage, he used to sing her silly love songs and promise her things no mortal could give—the moon and the stars, an uncloudy day, and eternal love. During their time together, he did his best to ensure they had a good life. The longer they stayed together, the more they felt a timeless comfort in each other's presence. It was as if they had known each other for all eternity.

They created two beautiful children together. Calvin was the firstborn. Hannah felt the child growing inside her before she got confirmation of the pregnancy. Calvin, the product of their passion, represented their flesh and spirit intertwined. He was their offering to eternity. They spoiled him in all the ways that mattered and did their best to protect him from the ugly horror of the world. Denise, their second child, had inherited her father's good bones and her mother's fearlessness and curiosity about life. The children were both teenagers now. Hannah often cringed when she thought about the challenges the world would throw at them.

###

If it was August, it was time for the family's getaway to their timeshare in Florida. When Calvin and Denise were young, the Bowie family had frequented Disneyworld and Universal Studios many times. The kids had gone to the Magic Kingdom when Calvin was still small enough to need a stroller, and Denise was a babe in arms. Denise dressed as Princess Tiana, complete with a pint-sized gown, crown, and wand. Her face lit up with joy when she met Minnie Mouse and Snow White for the first time. Hannah and Phillip accompanied the children on the rollercoasters until they were tall enough to ride alone.

Every year when the kids were young, Hannah was determined to stay for the light parade, which proved spectacular. As dusk fell, the park streets burst into life with colorful lights that danced and twinkled in sync with the music. The Light Parade dazzled onlookers with its charming Disney characters, such as Mickey Mouse, Minnie Mouse, Goofy, and Donald Duck, all decked out in their finest attire and shining brightly with the help of LED lights. The characters moved and danced along the parade route, interacting with the crowd and spreading joy and cheer to all who watched. When Hannah and her family returned home after the parade, everyone was overwhelmed by the sensory overload. On every trip, the family indulged in too much food and spent ample time under the sun, which left everyone cranky.

Denise's birthday was approaching, and Hannah relished celebrating in Orlando. Hannah realized that once her schedule picked up at the hospital, she would only have a few opportunities for a vacation. They traveled to Disney World in August. Calvin and Denise were old enough to explore the park independently as teenagers, so they agreed to meet Hannah and Phillip for lunch at one of the dining pavilions. Phillip stood in line to get refreshments for the family while Hannah watched for an available table in the crowded pavilion. When a table came open, Hannah rushed over and claimed the space, intending to hold it for the family. She found a cloth and began wiping the table.

"Look, Mom," a little White girl squealed with delight. "That lady is cleaning off a table for us."

Hannah resisted the urge to say something as she continued to prepare the table for Phillip, Calvin, and Denise when they arrived.

###

When Hannah was ten years old, her mother worked "down the line" as a domestic housekeeper in the homes of affluent White families. The compensation for her mother's labor was modest, which meant that their wardrobe mainly consisted of second-hand clothes, either handed down from the local mission or donated by the well-off residents of the North Side. As winter approached, Hannah had outgrown her clothes and needed a new coat.

One day, a wealthy lady her mother worked for gave her a coat. It was not just any coat; it was a plaid masterpiece, its green and tan squares perfectly aligned, crafted from the finest lamb's wool. This coat, a luxury item in its prime, represented the woman's generosity. Hannah's mother, gifted in tailoring, lovingly altered the coat by adjusting its hem, affixing new buttons, and ensuring it was freshly cleaned. Hannah's mother presented the coat to her daughter.

"I refuse to wear it," Hannah stubbornly declared.

The disappointment on her mother's face was evident. In response, her mother said, "You are a selfish and obstinate child," and reached for her leather belt, resorting to discipline as a last effort.

Despite the punishment, Hannah did not shed a tear. She remained resolute in her decision not to wear second-hand charity, especially from those who deemed her inferior and continually passed judgment. Her fierce independence and refusal to conform to societal expectations were unwavering. She was unwilling to negotiate her sense of identity and dignity.

###

Having returned home from their vacation, Phillip and the children had surrendered to sleep hours ago, yet a restless energy pulsed quietly within Hannah. From the chaise lounge on her screened-in porch, Hannah heard the distant murmur of the river in the night air. Enveloped by the night's embrace, Hannah cherished this time to process, reflect, connect, and regain balance; it was her usual time for profound meditation.

As the river's gentle whispers reached Hannah's ears, they seemed to carry with them the comforting presence of God, soothing the raw edges of her disappointment and the persistent sting of old resentments. The river's rhythmic flow, a constant undercurrent in the quiet of the night, reminded Hannah of her foremothers. Their lives, interwoven with her own through the fabric of time, shaped the essence of her being. In the velvety darkness, the spirits of her ancestors seemed to draw near, their silent strength mingling with her ceaseless search for inner peace. Hannah's relentless pursuit of new experiences, boundless curiosity, and deep-seated empathy were not merely traits but survival strategies, subtly forged in the fires of persistent sadness that dwelled deep within her soul.

Hannah thought of the generations of Black women before her, those who served as domestic workers in affluent households, their worth often overlooked, their labor undervalued. They endured long hours, low pay, and the dual burdens of discrimination and mistreatment, both at work and in society. Powerlessness, isolation, and a deep-seated yearning for respect marked their days as they navigated the intricate power dynamics and social hierarchies of their time. As the darkness of the evening wrapped around Hannah like a comforting shawl, the silence seemed to speak healing directly to her soul. The river's soft murmuring served as a backdrop to her thoughts, a soothing reminder of the continuous flow of life and the quiet strength that runs like a current through generations. It whispered of a path forward for healing and aiding others in navigating the tumultuous waters of life. Amen and Ashe.

2

2012 **Black Men Are Dying**

Hannah and Phillip were watching the news one February night in 2012 when the reporter announced a young man had been killed by a citizen in Sanford, Florida. Trayvon Martin, the seventeen-year-old Black student, was walking back to his father's fiancée's house in Sanford, Florida, after purchasing Skittles and a drink at a nearby convenience store. George Zimmerman, a neighborhood watch volunteer, spotted Martin and called the police, reporting him as a suspicious person. Zimmerman then began following Martin in his car and eventually got out to pursue him on foot. A confrontation ensued between the two, with Zimmerman claiming that Martin attacked him, leading to Zimmerman shooting Martin in self-defense. Martin was unarmed at the time of the shooting.

In the days following the murder, the news reported conflicting accounts of what exactly happened during the confrontation. Zimmerman sustained injuries to his head and face, which he claimed were caused by Martin. In contradiction, Martin's family and supporters argued that Zimmerman racially profiled and provoked Martin. Zimmerman claimed he shot Martin in self-defense after an altercation between the two. The details of the argument between Zimmerman and Martin remained unclear, as there were no definitive witnesses to provide a complete account of the events leading up to the shooting.

The ensuing outrage and protests spread throughout Lewis Town and around the nation, as many believed Martin's death was a result of racial profiling and unjustified use of force. The case sparked national debates on race, gun laws, and the criminal justice system. Zimmerman was initially not charged with any crime, citing Florida's "Stand Your Ground" law, which allows individuals to use deadly force if they feel threatened. However, after intense pressure from the public, Zimmerman was eventually charged with second-degree murder and manslaughter. In July 2013, Zimmerman was acquitted of all charges by a jury, further fueling the controversy surrounding the case.

Hannah, along with other mothers, feared for their children's lives. Even though Indigo had no children, she was around teenagers every day. Hannah needed to connect with her friend to figure out what to do. Indigo had prepared soup, salad, and garlic bread twists for lunch. Now, the two friends sat across from each other at Indigo's kitchen table as they began to speak about the Martin case; their voices were tinged with frustration.

"Trayvon's death threw everything off balance for me," Indigo confessed, looking down into her coffee as if seeking answers in its dark swirls. "Every part of me feels anger."

Hannah offered a reassuring nod.

"Me, too. It's like Trayvon Martin was metaphorically lynched, and Zimmerman just walks away. How can there be any justice in that?" Hannah queried.

"It's a hard pill to swallow, Hannah. It challenges my understanding of justice. The suffering and evil that plague the Black community—it's like a dark cloud that never lifts."

In Lewis Town, tensions ran high, with sentiments often fraught with anger, fear, and resentment. The divide between different ideological groups fed deep-seated hatred and mistrust, fueling a cycle of suspicion and violence.

Peace eluded Hannah, Indigo, and other members of their racially and economically divided community. In the wake of Trayvon Martin's death, subtle acts of discrimination lost their camouflage as the harsh light of anger shed light on systemic racism and unequal treatment in various aspects of life among marginalized groups. In contrast, many of those in the privileged group hid behind ignorance, apathy, or even hostility, entertaining feelings of entitlement, superiority, and indifference toward the struggles of people they had marginalized. On the other hand, some formerly blinded by their privilege regained clarity on the injustices and cried out in solidarity with their neighbors.

###

The Bowie family grew weary of their annual visits to theme parks and timeshares in Orlando. After owning the Florida timeshare for many years, the novelty of visiting the same location year after year wore off. Increasing HOA fees had also become burdensome. Moreover, the attractions in Orlando had lost their allure after multiple visits. Without fresh and thrilling adventures to anticipate, the family was looking for a new vacation destination.

Hannah began to explore other properties owned by their timeshare company. One was in Branson, a town in southwest Missouri known as a family vacation spot. Nestled in the Ozark mountains, the resort boasted theaters, live shows, and relaxation. After reading the promo brochure, Hannah and Phillip decided to check it out. They were just about ready to book a week at the resort when the NAACP issued a travel advisory for Missouri. Michael Brown had been murdered by police in Ferguson, not too far from the resort.

###

Michael Brown, an eighteen-year-old Black man, was shot and killed by Darren Wilson, a White police officer, on August 9, 2014, in Ferguson, Missouri. The incident reignited national conversations about police brutality, racial profiling, and the treatment of Black people by law enforcement. The backlash led to the formation of the Black Lives Matter movement and called for systemic changes in policing and criminal justice. Widespread protests and civil unrest erupted in Ferguson and across the United States.

Preceding the shooting, Brown and his friend Dorian Johnson were walking in the middle of the street when Officer Wilson approached them in his patrol car and told them to move to the sidewalk. An altercation ensued between Brown and Wilson, leading to Wilson firing several shots at Brown, fatally injuring him. During the shooting, conflicting witness accounts emerged, with some claiming that Brown had his hands up in surrender when he was shot, while others said he was charging at Wilson. The police initially claimed that Brown had assaulted Wilson and tried to grab his gun, prompting Wilson to use lethal force in self-defense. Following the shooting, protests erupted in Ferguson, with demonstrators demanding justice for Brown and calling for accountability in policing. The protests were met with heavy police response, including the use of tear gas and militarized tactics, further escalating tensions in the community.

Many impressionable young people were deeply affected by the events surrounding Michael Brown's death, including young men and women in Lewis Town and around the country. For some high school students and recent graduates, the riots sparked anger and frustration at the injustice they perceived, which led to increased activism. The riots also caused fear and anxiety among students. The violence and unrest left a lasting impact on their mental health and sense of safety.

###

The news of yet another senseless killing of a young Black man by law enforcement filled Hannah with a deep sense of outrage and frustration. She could not fathom the injustice of a system that repeatedly failed to hold those in power accountable for their actions. Hannah's heart ached for Michael Brown's family, for the mother who had lost her son in such a violent and unjust manner. The lack of transparency in the investigation only fueled her rage further, as it seemed like those responsible for his death would never face the consequences of their actions.

Many subsequent incidents occurred in which police brutalized young Black men, oppressing them for minor infractions of the law. One particularly egregious example was the case of Eric Garner in New York City. In July 2014, Garner, a forty-three-year-old Black man, was approached by police officers for allegedly selling loose cigarettes on the street, a minor offense. Despite Garner posing no threat and repeatedly stating that he could not breathe, an officer placed him in a chokehold, leading to his death.

Another instance of police brutality involved Freddie Gray in Baltimore. In April 2015, Gray, a twenty-five-year-old Black man, was arrested for possessing a switchblade knife, a charge that was later found to be inaccurate. During his arrest, Gray sustained a severe spinal cord injury while in police custody, ultimately leading to his death. His mistreatment at the hands of law enforcement sparked outrage and protests in Baltimore and beyond.

Additionally, the case of Philando Castile in Falcon Heights, Minnesota, on July 6, 2016, highlighted the excessive force used by police against the young Black man. Castile, a thirty-two-year-old Black man, was pulled over for a broken taillight. Despite complying with the officer's orders and informing him that he had a legal firearm in the car, Castile was shot and killed in front of his girlfriend and her young daughter. The incident, captured on video and shared widely on social media, reignited national debates about police brutality and racial profiling.

The ongoing brutality underscored the systemic issues of racism and excessive use of force within law enforcement that disproportionately affect young Black men. In Lewis Town, Hannah joined protests and rallies, raising her voice alongside others who shared her pain. Despite the overwhelming emotions that consumed her, Hannah channeled her wrath into action, fighting for change and standing in solidarity with those who refused to be silent in the face of injustice. The fury that simmered within her was a powerful force, driving her to speak out and demand accountability for the lives lost to police violence.

###

In the dim light of early morning, Hannah sat motionless, her heart carrying burdens so heavy she felt like she would drown. The porch was silent, save for the soft rustling of pages as she turned them slowly, deliberately. In these moments of desperation, she felt a nudge towards the Book of Exodus—a beacon of God's mighty acts and unwavering support. For Hannah, the story of the parting of the Red Sea stood as a towering pillar of hope, liberation, redemption, and Divine authority. It was her sanctuary, her refuge when the shadows of doubt crept too close. This ancient narrative of miraculous deliverance reminded her that even in the face of overwhelming adversity, God's hand was ever-present, molding the impossible into escape pathways.

Despite biblical miracles, the present-day world grew darker and more hostile. Both seen and unseen forces conspired to rewrite the truths she held dear, presenting a narrative spun with deceit and malice. It was as if the very dream killers from her community were no longer content with stifling voices but were now intent on erasing the very essence of their history, their identity. Hannah knew that to discern the truth, she must look back as the Sankofa bird does—acknowledging her heritage and the depth of her struggle. She clung to the belief that God was sovereign, orchestrating events from above with a vast and intricate perspective that human minds could scarcely comprehend. Each story of Exodus, where God turned despair into deliverance, fortified her resolve. She believed that, despite appearances, God had a master plan.

Exhaustion clawed at her, threatening to drag her into despair. Her spirit felt sapped, but her faith implored her to stand firm—to plug into the divine power source that had fueled generations before her. She felt it was time to marshal her gifts, those bestowed upon her by a gracious God. It was time to take up her literal and spiritual staff and prepare to witness the deliverance she knew was coming. Her heart was heavy to the point of breaking. Yet, precisely at this breaking point, she stretched her faith, ready to flex against the tides of adversity. With every fiber of her being, Hannah believed in the God who would show up and part the vast Red Seas of injustice that threatened to drown her people in despair. Hannah endured with staff in hand, eyes on the horizon, waiting for the waters to part. Amen and Ashe.

3

2016 Lenten Service

It was February 2016. Indigo invited Hannah to attend a Lenten program at her church. The speakers that night echoed the ideas of theologian James Cone. Hannah often struggled to make sense of Cone's comparison of the cross to the lynching tree. From her seminary studies, Hannah recalled Cone suggesting that Black suffering in the form of "lynching" resulted in the emergence of a resilient Black faith. As she recalled, Cone also asserted that there was something redemptive about suffering.

Hannah cringed at the thought. The only redemption she could see in this situation was that suffering represented an opportunity to hold up a mirror of accountability in the face of the oppressors. The speakers that night also discussed resurrection. They suggested that for something to be resurrected, it must first die and be buried—no cross or crown. The speakers avowed that justice-minded people must engage in discussions about what died and was buried on the day these young Black men were interred. Hannah pursued that line of thinking. What exactly was resurrected because these Black young men lost their lives to violence in a racist America? Hannah was preoccupied with the thoughts of Emmitt Till, Trayvon Martin, and Michael Brown, whose crosses consisted of being Black in a racist America.

As Hannah further contemplated the suffering of mothers who had lost their young children to street violence, she realized that Calvin fell into the age range of many of the victims. The thought terrified her that she might join the woeful cries one day. The senseless killings struck her as a heartbreaking, mind-blowing, and devastating manifestation of suffering. Standing in solidarity with other mothers, Hannah overwhelmingly desired to call out for mercy and justice.

###

After the program, Hannah and Indigo resumed their analysis over coffee in the church basement. As they continued, the hum of conversations around them imparted a sense of shared urgency.

"I don't understand how we find redemption in the suffering. How do we affirm our faith when our brothers and sisters are being metaphorically lynched and crucified in a society that still harbors so much hatred?" Indigo asked.

Hannah sipped her coffee. "That's the ongoing struggle. Part of our theodicy is our justification of God in the face of evil. It feels like a constant test of faith, trying to find meaning and justice in all this pain."

"Yes," Indigo responded, "and perhaps our faith and these discussions are part of navigating through it. By questioning, by wrestling with these hard questions, maybe we're slowly moving toward some understanding, or at least a way to bear the weight."

"I hope so, Indigo. I do. Because without that hope, without that belief in eventual justice and redemption, what's the point of the struggle?"

"Right, Hannah. It's about holding onto that hope despite everything. And maybe our conversations and reflections are small steps toward healing and change."

When Hannah got home, she retreated to her quiet place to reflect. Many concerns emerged when she weighed the implications of redemption and resurrection. The NAACP had suggested that the premature death of young Black men served as a wake-up call, prompting Black families to confront the harsh realities of surviving in a racist society. They believed it compelled a reality check to distinguish lies from truths and to encourage critical thinking about identity. Hannah concurred with the NAACP's position.

Like many Christians, Hannah believed that the cross of Jesus was redemptive, and the redemption occurred as part of a three-part process. First, Jesus had to suffer and die. He had to be buried. And then he had to be resurrected for the vile act of crucifixion to take on redemptive meaning. When taken together, the three parts of the passion resulted in a synergy where the whole was greater than the sum of its parts. Because of this three-part act of love, victory triumphed over death and redemption over sin. Hence, there was power in the resurrection. Now, the God Hannah served was a God of justice. Justice demanded that something be born again from the precious seeds of young bodies planted too soon amid so much sorrow. So, what exactly must be resurrected when young people lose their lives to senseless violence?

For one thing, Hannah believed that conversations had to be resurrected. Some people suggested that the deaths of these young people had awakened the need for families and friends to have frank discussions with one another. There was a need for tableside chats about the brutal realities of survival in a hostile society. We needed to pass down survival skills that our foremothers and forefathers learned about in complex, mean, and evil times. Survival skills had to be passed down from father to son, mother to daughter, sister to sister, brother to brother, and generation to generation.

What else? Consciousness needed to be raised. There was already evidence of it on the horizon. Marchers were protesting across the nation. Lights were being shed on the darkness of unjust laws and lopsided enforcement. People were digging deep to find the courage to hold public forums and grapple with the hard questions that had to be addressed.

What else? Mirrors must be held up—mirrors of accountability forcing perpetrators and victims alike to scrutinize the root causes of violence, injustice, and other critical concerns. Lovers of truth should start to examine racism and poverty under a super-powered microscope. Prophets like Habakkuk exposed what had been undercover for too long and advised us to make the inconsistencies plain so that a runner could read them!

What else? Oh, yes! Math skills needed to be refreshed! The death of these young people has forced us to check our reality and double-check our math. We need a refresher course to help us understand that there are no "greater" and "lesser" human beings. No people are three-fifths human or some other arbitrary fraction of the whole. All people are made in God's image! We are members of the same humanity for whom Christ died—once and for all. And because the "error" term—the Eternal term –reconciles all, we must now join in with the indignant and passionate cries of mothers who had lost their children to violence. Because there is a Synergistic term, we must have hope and renewed confidence that justice will prevail! Because there is a Sacred term, we must stand up, individually and collectively, and shout, there is power in the blood!

###

Later that year, Indigo's church invited Hannah to deliver a sermon for Advent, which should have been a season anticipating hope, peace, joy, and love. For many people, the preceding year was like passing through the badlands before getting to the good lands. Entering Advent was like entering a wilderness where there is unspeakable hatred. As Hannah prepared for the sermon, she began thinking about Dylan Roof, who last year, on June 17, 2015, killed nine people in an act of violence at the Mother Emmanuel African Methodist Episcopal Church in Charleston, South Carolina. He opened fire during a prayer service that police now describe as a "hate crime." Hannah also recalled the recent mistrial of the police officer who killed Walter Scott—again in South Carolina. Walter Scott was a devout Christian who sang in his church choir. He was stopped for driving with a broken taillight and ran away from the officer, who shot him in the back. Even though the incident was captured on video, justice did not prevail. Walter Scott's life was cheapened, and racism was working overtime that day. Other victims came to mind:

Dantrell Davis. 1992. Seven years old. He was walking to school with his mother in the Cabrini-Green housing project when he was shot to death by a sniper aiming for someone else.

Eric Morse. 1994. Five years old. He was killed when two boys, ages ten and eleven, dropped him out of a fourteenth-floor window in an Ida B. Wells high-rise because he wouldn't steal candy for them.

Ryan Harris. 1998. Eleven years old. She set off one day to ride her bike in her South Side neighborhood of Englewood. Her body was found a day later in an isolated backyard.

Blair Holt. 2007. Sixteen years old. Shot to death while riding a CTA bus on the far South Side. He was trying to protect someone else.

Derrion Albert. 2009. Sixteen years old. Beaten to death with a railroad tie by several boys near his high school in the Roseland neighborhood.

Jonylah Watkins. 2013. Six months old. She was shot to death in the Woodlawn neighborhood by a man allegedly aiming for her father while her father sat next to her in a minivan.

Hadiya Pendleton. 2014. Fifteen years old. Shot in a South Side play lot—did you hear me—a play lot. It was a case of mistaken identity.

Eric Garner. Alton Sterling. Rakia Boyd. Freddie Gray. Sandra Bland. Laquan McDonald. Have mercy, Jesus.

There were too many names of the dead to pronounce in this brief sermon. All Hannah could think about was the unspeakable sorrow surrounding the loss of these precious lives in the wilderness, many of them victims of the climate of violence that plagues our communities.

She went on the porch to sit near Phillip, for she had lost her writing inspiration. As the evening light faded and cast shadows around the space, Hannah sat beside Phillip, her eyes reflecting a storm of emotions. Phillip, a man of few words, watched her with attentive eyes, ready to offer the silent strength she often leaned on.

"Phillip," Hannah began, her voice shaky, "do you ever wonder what it's like for a parent to lose a child?" She paused, swallowing hard. "I've been reading stories, and they all say the pain and sadness never disappear. It just becomes less frequent over time."

Phillip nodded, his face a mask of concern as he listened.

"At first," she continued, "parents cry endlessly. Eventually, they reach a point where they can smile at the memories of their lost child. There's this deep yearning, though. One parent said if they could see their child again, even in a dream, it might bring some comfort."

Phillip put his arm around her. His touch was gentle and grounding. Hannah sighed, pressing on despite the heaviness in her heart.

"They say things get worse before they get better. Like, the sky is darkest before the dawn, or you have to hit bottom to start looking up again." She looked at Phillip, her eyes searching for some affirmation. "But honestly, I'm struggling to see evidence that we're approaching the dawn."

Phillip squeezed her shoulder, a silent symbol of his presence and support. Hannah's thoughts drifted to her upcoming sermon.

"And now, I have to talk about the joy of the Advent season. What is joy, really? It's supposed to be more than just happiness. Some say it's the fulfillment of hope, the end of trials, coming back home after a long journey." She trailed off, her voice tinged with doubt.

"Do you remember that song, 'Unspeakable Joy'? That term, *unspeakable*, means you can't even put it into words," Hannah mused, looking beyond Phillip as if trying to visualize the concept. "But right now, joy feels like a foreign language."

Understanding her need to process these heavy thoughts aloud, Phillip remained silent but attentive.

"And then there's this other thing bothering me," she added, her tone shifting slightly as she touched upon another deep issue. "The plight of Black youths in many urban environments. It's like they're living in a wilderness, where everything that could help them grow has been stripped away by corruption and apathy. It's a harsh landscape, filled with dangers that can stifle their potential and aspirations."

As the conversation wound down to a close, Phillip finally spoke, his voice soft yet firm. "Hannah, I may not have all the answers, but I'm here with you through this wilderness, the waiting, and the uncertainty. We'll find that dawn together."

Hannah nodded, a tear slipping down her cheek, comforted by the assurance that, though the path was unclear, she was not walking it alone.

After Hannah went back inside, she put aside her notes. She would pick them up later. Her heart was broken because justice was still delayed. She closed her eyes and prayed for strength to go through the wilderness, wastelands, and deserts. She prayed for fortification to await in the spirit of Advent for peace and unspeakable joy. She drifted to sleep, imagining she was in a dust storm.

###

Hannah imagined a massive cloud rising before her, extending high into the sky and sprawling across the horizon. She thought she heard voices, but they were only the wind beckoning her to pause amidst the fury of the dust storm of injustice. A cloud cast a rapid shadow, dimming the day into a sudden twilight. Born from the echoes of trauma, Hannah's internal storms brewed deep emotional and spiritual turmoil within her, weaving through her threads of depression and despair. The relentless winds of poverty had battered her life with the chilling cold of hatred and the deep, entangled roots of structural and systemic racism. Sometimes, these storms overwhelmed her spirit, leaving her feeling numb and inadequate.

In those moments of inner turmoil, Hannah embraced stillness. She decided to let the metaphorical dust settle around her. She found wisdom in steering off the path to let the tempest pass. When she awakened, she would gather her thoughts, reflect deeply, engage in the purifying act of fasting, and deepen her prayers. She would navigate the complexities with the patience and persistence with which water shaped the earth. She would embrace the time of stillness to find clarity and strength in the calm after the storm as she prepared to continue her renewed journey. Amen and Ashe.

4

2016 **Reginald La Rue Chambers**

The house was dark as she pulled into the driveway. Indigo was halfway through the door when the telephone rang.

"Indigo, this is Hannah. Reggie was involved in a car accident. Can you come to the hospital right away?"

Upon her arrival, the EMT briefed Indigo on the situation.

"Hello, Mrs. Chambers," the EMT began. "Witnesses say your husband was headed north toward the riverfront. Police officers stopped him because his taillight was broken. They approached him and told him to get out of the car. Your husband asked the officers why they had stopped him and refused to comply with their instructions. The police said your husband moved toward them with a threatening posture. Witnesses say your husband kept asking the officers what he had done wrong. That's when one police officer threw him to the ground and told him he was resisting arrest. The officers beat him with their nightsticks, hitting him in the head repeatedly. Reggie sustained extensive damage to his skull. He's in CT now."

"Thank you," Indigo responded to the EMT.

Hannah waited in the consultation room with Indigo until the doctors were ready to give an update on Reggie's condition. While they waited, Indigo shared part of their family story.

This wasn't the first concussion Reggie had suffered. One Saturday, he hitchhiked across town to attend a party where heavy drinking ensued, and the atmosphere was charged. At some point, Reggie stepped out onto the wooden porch for air. Whether out of retaliation or by accident, someone pushed him over the railing of the third-floor porch. He landed on his head, sustained brain injuries, and fell into a coma, though he later recovered.

"Do you have family or friends you can call to support you and Reggie during this?" Hannah inquired.

"I have no family. It's pretty much just me. But many friends from church are willing to help, and I have my colleagues from school. And I have you."

"I'm here for you if you need me," Hannah reassured her friend.

After an hour, a doctor and his resident entered the room to speak with Indigo.

###

"Mrs. Chambers," the doctor announced, addressing Indigo, "Your husband sustained damage to his head. He has a skull fracture and some contusions. We suspect that he might have a traumatic brain injury (TBI), but we have to wait a couple of days to confirm. Do you have any questions for me?"

"What exactly is a traumatic brain injury?" Indigo asked.

"The injury has two levels—the primary injury results from an external force, usually a violent blow to the head. Immediate or delayed symptoms may include confusion, blurry vision, and difficulty concentrating. The secondary injury occurs later and may involve swelling and increased intracranial pressure. Often, we don't see evidence of these injuries during the initial CT scan. We will know more in two to three days. We will transfer him to the ICU and keep a close watch. We're waiting for a bed now. Would you like to see him?"

"Will you come with me, Hannah?" Indigo asked.

"Of course," Hannah responded.

When Indigo laid eyes on her husband, she gasped for air. Reggie seemed to be unconscious, with bandages on his head and face. Visible signs of trauma, including bruising, swelling, and cuts, were apparent. He was connected to machines and monitors that tracked vital signs and brain activity. The critical care team had placed a breathing tube to assist with oxygen support. An IV line was inserted for medication and fluids. Reggie was unresponsive to the sounds in the room, nor did he respond when Indigo touched his hand. His mind had retreated to a place where her words could not reach him. Hannah and Indigo prayed silently that God would be present with Reggie's spirit.

"This is worse than the last time he had a concussion," Indigo remarked.

The critical care team allowed Indigo to spend the night in the ICU; she slept in a chair beside Reggie's bed and prayed.

After about a week, due to the extraordinary medical interventions, Reggie was well enough to be moved from the ICU to one of the medical units, where he would begin inpatient rehabilitation. Reggie demanded Indigo's full attention. Indigo mustered the strength to deal gracefully and patiently with Reggie's mood swings and outbursts. Reggie's sullen and ill-tempered behavior was testing Indigo's limits once again. Throughout their marriage, there were numerous occasions when Indigo felt tempted to leave. As far as Indigo was concerned, Reggie's worst shortcoming was his intense jealousy. On multiple instances, after observing Indigo merely talking to other men—not even sitting close, just engaging in conversation—he would conclude that she was having an affair and would sleep on the couch as a form of retaliation. Indigo had never entertained the thought of being unfaithful. She was devoted to Reggie, and her Baptist upbringing strictly forbade extramarital affairs. Despite that, she stayed by Reggie's side, visiting him daily and advocating for his needs with the medical team. As Reggie slowly improved, he showed signs of his old self. Somewhere in her mind, Indigo hoped that this traumatic experience would bring them closer together and help Reggie overcome his past behaviors.

###

Having a traumatic brain injury significantly impacted Reggie's physical, cognitive, emotional, and behavioral functioning. Reggie's rehabilitation journey was long and involved a team of professionals—physical, occupational, speech, and cognitive rehabilitation specialists. As days turned into weeks, Reggie and Indigo began to navigate the complex aftermath of his injury, confronting various challenges that reshaped their everyday existence. Reggie's physical symptoms were persistent headaches that throbbed mercilessly, dizziness, fatigue, off-balance, and new sensitivities to light and sound, turning ordinary environments into sensory battlegrounds. Motor difficulties also surfaced, making simple tasks feel monumental. As his physical recovery progressed slowly, more profound changes began to emerge.

Reggie's cognitive functions were impaired, affecting his memory, concentration, and problem-solving skills. Emotionally and behaviorally, Reggie began experiencing irritability, was quick to anger, and was prone to sudden sadness. His relationships began to suffer as friends and church family had to tread carefully, unsure which version of Reggie they would encounter. Communication also became challenging as Reggie struggled to find the right words, often pausing mid-sentence. Once enjoyable conversations now felt exhausting, leaving him more isolated and misunderstood. Amid these trials, coping strategies such as setting realistic goals, celebrating small victories, participating in support groups, and family care were crucial. Despite the profound changes to his life, with the proper support and indomitable spirit, Reggie began to carve out a new path, each step forward a testament to his resilience.

###

Indigo screamed joyfully when she learned Reggie was medically stable enough to return home with a specialized rehab program. They resided on the ground level of an old three-flat building near the intersection where north and south formed a separating line. It was one of the few buildings spared during urban renewal. Their home was a vintage construction with high ceilings, crown molding, and many built-in surprises like the breakfront near the back of the house by the kitchen. Indigo adored the wall of built-in shelves, where she placed the dishes she had purchased at Big Lots for ninety-nine cents each. She kept the China and silver pieces inherited from her grandmother on the top shelf. Reggie spent most of his time in the living room at the front of the house, featuring a built-in gas fireplace, a hardwood mantelpiece, and a clear street view.

The property required significant TLC and renovations to meet ADA compliance standards. The family's insurance program covered some of the costs. The furnace, skylight, and water heater needed repairs. The building required tuckpointing, and numerous carpentry projects were still pending. The painting was a constant endeavor. Before his accident, Reggie was accustomed to making minor repairs himself. Now, his attempts at fixing things often did more harm than good. Reggie began to feel he was taking up more space than he deserved and promising more than he could deliver. Indigo contacted a home health care service to provide extra support now that Reggie was home.

Their marriage vows included a commitment to devotion "until death," so they cared for each other during good health and illness. Indigo managed everything for him—laundry, groceries, house cleaning, bill paying, and all the errands. She cooked special meals and spoon-fed him when he was in the mood. When it was time for his physical therapy, she drove him there and assisted him with his home exercises.

As soon as they were given clearance to travel, they recuperated at the Wisconsin Dells in the off-season. Limited mobility curtailed their ability to explore the attractions fully. With time on their hands, they sat on the deck and watched local birds snatch up the crumbs they tossed. Most Sundays, they were accustomed to watching NFL football on TV. To their dismay, local Wisconsin channels blacked out the game between the Chicago Bears and the Green Bay Packers. They opted to watch home improvement shows on HGTV instead.

###

As the sun dipped below the horizon, casting a soft glow through the window, Indigo sat at her kitchen table and slumped in her chair. She was weary, both in body and spirit, the kind of exhaustion that seeps into your bones and settles there, heavy and unyielding. In the solitude of the evening, her thoughts drifted to a memory that always managed to bring tears to her eyes, a sorrowful echo of a dream that once filled her heart with hope.

In her younger years, when life seemed to brim with possibilities, Indigo had envisioned a bustling household filled with the laughter and chaos of children. She remembered how, in those days, her circle of friends was always abuzz with talks of pregnancies and babies. They passed around maternity clothes and swapped cribs as if these were mere tokens of a shared dream she, too, was destined to experience. But as the years passed, that path had grown thorny and painful for Indigo.

The journey to motherhood, which she anticipated with such enthusiasm, turned into a saga of medical consultations, tests, and growing despair. She recalled the sharp sting of needles and the cold, impersonal touch of ultrasound probes. After two relentless years of trying, the verdict that her fallopian tubes were blocked and fibroids marred her womb felt like a cruel sentence. The surgery that followed, filled with the promise of a solution, only led to further heartbreak. The laparoscopic procedure failed, and the doctor's words had been a sterile, blunt instrument severing her hopes: there was no chance for her to conceive.

As the reality of her situation sank in, grief enveloped her and Reggie, a shared cloak they wore silently. Yet, in those days of recovery, Reggie had been her unwavering support. He had tended to her with a tenderness she remembered now in vivid detail. He would wake early to prepare breakfast, and they would eat together, quietly enjoying the simple meals he could cook. Reggie bathed her when she was too weak, carefully changed her dressings, and meticulously kept their home clean, creating a sanctuary where she could heal. Night after night, he lay beside her, comforting against the chill that no blanket could entirely ward off. His steady and calm breath often lulled her into a fitful sleep, where dreams of what could have been danced just out of reach.

As Indigo sat alone, the weight of those unfulfilled dreams pressed heavily upon her. She felt a profound sadness for Reggie, who, in his diminished state, could no longer remember those days of quiet bravery, of love spoken in acts of care and devotion. Tears streamed down her cheeks, not just for the children they never had but for the memories that time was erasing from the man who had stood by her when her own body had betrayed her. Indigo mourned in the quiet twilight of her kitchen, enveloped by the shadows of what might have been. Amen and Ashe.

5

2017 **Changed Forever**

Reggie remained in home rehab for months, taking a long time to regain his cognitive awareness and physical strength. He was eager to test his handyman skills, but Indigo knew his failures would only enhance his helplessness and frustration. He drifted through his days, often unaware of what he was bumping into, creating more messes than he fixed. His social life had diminished significantly. Before the accident, he was heavily involved in church clubs and undertook fixer-upper projects around the sanctuary. It comforted Reggie when congregation members occasionally stopped by to see him, cheering him up with homemade desserts and stories of the good old days. However, Reggie could not interact with them effectively due to his diminished cognitive abilities, and he was only sometimes on his best behavior when visitors came.

With the assistance of therapists, Indigo devised a plan to increase Reggie's positive behaviors and decrease inappropriate ones. They displayed rules and protocols on a magnet board in the kitchen. They encouraged him to engage in enjoyable activities, which increased Reggie's sense of autonomy and stimulated his creativity. Surprisingly, Reggie discovered a talent for watercolors. He started watching the National Geographic Channel, particularly enjoying shows about rivers. After each episode, he gathered his art supplies and began to paint. Initially, his renditions were messy. With time and the help of his art therapist, his pictures took on breadth, depth, and movement, telling the stories he struggled to express verbally. After several months, Reggie created numerous scenes depicting the rivers' remarkable character. Initially, he hung them in his den, but later, he began giving them to visitors as tokens of his affection.

###

The changes in Reggie's sensory processing were the most obvious. Colors appeared more vivid than before; each hue imbued with an almost tangible depth. Textures called to him, whispering secrets of their essence that he had never heard before. This heightened sensitivity was overwhelming and illuminative, pushing him to pour these novel sensory experiences into his art, transforming his traditional landscapes into surreal, vibrant expressions that pulsed with new life. In the quiet solitude of his studio, Reggie stared at the blank canvas before him. As he dipped his brush into the paint, he was about to transfer color onto canvas to explore the profound scenes within his mind and soul.

Emotionally, Reggie found himself in uncharted waters. His emotions surged and dipped unpredictably, painting his world in stark, intense shades. Happiness was euphoric, sadness was abyssal, and anger was all-consuming. This new emotional depth did not just alter his life experience; it seeped into his art, making each piece a raw, unfiltered conduit of his feelings. His canvases became the arena where he battled and embraced his amplified emotions, each brush stroke capturing a fragment of his transformed emotional landscape.

The brain injury disrupted his conventional thinking patterns. Where once there was a systematic approach to his art, there lay a path marked by unusual associations and creative leaps. Problems that would have stumped him before now sparked unconventional solutions. This shift opened a floodgate of creativity, and Reggie found himself experimenting with new techniques and mediums, each piece a testament to his evolving artistic identity.

Symbolism, too, took on a new meaning in his work. What previously seemed like straightforward concepts now danced with ambiguity and depth. Simple images morphed into complex metaphors, each infused with personal significance and reflecting his inner turmoil and revelations post-injury. His art became a dialogue of symbols, each piece a more profound commentary on his journey through recovery and self-discovery.

Resilience became a core theme in his life and art. The act of creating became both a refuge and a method of exploration, a physical manifestation of his inner strength and evolving perspective.

Indigo watched as Reggie painted one of his creations, a picture of a tranquil river. The sun gently kissed the water's surface, reflecting the golden hues of the autumn foliage in a peaceful scene. As she gazed at the painting, Indigo could imagine the crisp, cool air carrying the faint scent of fallen leaves and the gentle sound of rustling trees. The river flowed steadily, its surface shimmering in the sunlight as small ripples danced to the movement of the current.

Another painting depicted the river in a rich blue-green shade, so clear that one could see the smooth stones lining the riverbed below. Fish darted in and out of the shadows, their sleek bodies glinting in the sunlight as they navigated the gentle currents. Indigo felt as if she could almost hear birds chirping and fluttering overhead, their calls blending harmoniously with the soothing rush of the river. Tall grasses swayed in the breeze along the banks, their golden stalks bending like a graceful dance. Trees stood tall and proud, their branches adorned with red, orange, and gold leaves.

Many of Reggie's portraits showed the angry face of the river. In one portrait, the river was at flood stage. The raging current uprooted and carried away trees along the banks. Debris and branches were swept downstream, creating a dangerous situation for anyone caught in the waters. The wind howled and whipped through the trees, adding to the storm's chaos. Rain poured down in sheets, soaking everything in its path. Indigo could almost hear the sound of the loud storm drowning out any other noise in the area. Despite the danger and destruction, there was a certain beauty in the power of nature on display. A companion portrait showed the aftermath of the flood. As quickly as the storm had begun, it passed, leaving behind a scene of devastation. The river slowly receded, the waters calming and returning to normal.

###

A brain injury can interfere with one's decision-making and executive functioning, which is responsible for planning, organizing, problem-solving, decision-making, and self-regulation. Before the accident, Reggie was known for his sharp wit and ability to effortlessly manage multiple projects. Now, he was trapped in a fog that muddled his thoughts and clouded his judgment. Planning and organizing, once as natural to him as breathing, now felt like foreign concepts—each attempt to set goals or prioritize tasks ended in frustration, with Reggie feeling overwhelmed and defeated. The simple act of starting a project was daunting, let alone seeing it through to completion.

Judgment, once a pillar of his personality, now seemed compromised. Reggie found it increasingly difficult to assess risks and anticipate the consequences of his actions. Each decision was a gamble, as if he were playing a game of chance without understanding the rules. Perhaps most troubling was Reggie's loss of self-awareness. Reggie's insight into his condition was blurred, making it difficult to recognize these changes in himself. This lack of awareness meant he often saw the errors in his thinking or the flawed logic behind his decisions when it was too late.

One day, Reggie ran out of black paint during one of his art projects. Everyone knows that black is an essential color in the creation of visual art for several reasons. Black is an intense color that contrasts sharply with lighter colors. This contrast can help to create depth and dimension in a piece of artwork. Black can emphasize some aspects of a composition by drawing the viewer's attention to specific areas. It can also be used to create a focal point in an artwork. Black is often associated with darkness, mystery, and drama. Artists can use black to convey a certain mood or evoke a specific emotional response from the viewer. Finally, black can define shapes and forms within a composition. It can outline objects or create boundaries between different elements in an artwork.

The art therapy team had taught Reggie to be independent and creative. Due to their excellent teaching, Reggie figured he now had the power to do things for himself. Reggie was convinced that he could not proceed without his black paint. No one was in the room with Reggie when he decided to walk to the store to replenish his supply of black pigment. Indigo had gone to the store, and the housekeeper was working on the week's laundry in the basement; Reggie decided to venture to the hardware store independently to purchase the needed supplies.

His only currency was his rare coin collection, which he kept in a box under his bed. He thought about telling the housekeeper about his planned trip but did not want to distract her. Taking a calculated risk, Reggie retrieved the coins, placed them in a gallon-size plastic bag, and headed to the store two blocks away, his bag of coins in full sight. He forgot to close the front door when he left the house. Feeling a sense of pride and accomplishment, he purchased his supplies, which he put in his backpack along with the leftover rare coins. Eager to return to his painting, he took a shortcut home through the park. The sun began to set, casting long shadows and bathing the surroundings in a warm, golden light. The gentle rustle of leaves and the distant chirping of birds created a surreal backdrop to the unfolding events.

###

As Reggie walked along the path, footsteps approaching from behind shattered the park's tranquility. The suddenness of the attack sent a jolt of fear through Reggie, and he turned to see a masked figure rushing toward him. A second masked man tried to grab Reggie's backpack while the first assailant tussled with Reggie on the ground for long seconds. One of the men tugged forcefully at the backpack, but Reggie refused to let it go. The scuffle that followed was chaotic, with Reggie struggling to hold onto his backpack as the assailants attempted to wrest it from his grasp.

The sounds of the struggle were chilling—the harsh grunts of the attackers, Reggie's desperate cries for help, and the sickening thud of blows landing on his body. The violence of the attack echoed through the park, a stark contrast to the peaceful surroundings that had once enveloped Reggie in a sense of security. The smell of freshly cut grass mingled with the metallic tang of blood as the attackers mercilessly kicked and hit Reggie, causing him to fall to the ground in a haze of pain and confusion. The fear and adrenaline in the air were palpable, adding to the sense of urgency and danger that permeated the scene.

The two assailants kicked Reggie repeatedly in the head and the stomach. Finally, one of them pulled out a gun and hit Reggie on the head with the butt of it. The strap on the backpack finally broke, allowing the man to grab the pack and run off, leaving Reggie battered and unconscious in the park. A sense of shock and disbelief hung heavy in the air.

The housekeeper was frantic when she realized Reggie had eloped. She immediately called 911 and Indigo. The police soon found Reggie lying in a park, unconscious, with the straps of a backpack clutched in his hand. At the scene, EMTs quickly attended to Reggie's wounds before transporting him to the hospital with sirens blaring.

###

When Indigo arrived at the hospital, she found Reggie in a coma. The familiar machines surrounding him buzzed and beeped, the lifelines keeping him alive. She sat beside Hannah, who had arrived to be with her friend to tarry and pray. Eventually, the doctors delivered the heartbreaking news that there was nothing more they could do for Reggie. The room was filled only with the soft swishing of the breathing machine and the subtle rise and fall of Reggie's chest as he breathed in and out. After consulting with her support group and church members, Indigo decided to withdraw Reggie from care. Church members and friends came to the hospital to stand vigil with her.

Around midnight, the atmosphere in the room shifted subtly. Indigo noticed that Reggie had stopped breathing. "He's gone," she whispered. The group shared a private, emotional moment, recognizing that Reggie had crossed a bridge to the next phase of his existence.

###

As the clock struck 6:00 p.m., the funeral directors organized the mourners, guiding them past the coffin to view the body and bid their farewells. They efficiently moved the lines along, allowing each group a brief moment with the deceased before ushering them forward. The church buzzed with the flutter of cardboard fans, and the deacon mothers, dressed in white, comforted those in the aisle seats with soft words of condolence, casting wary glances at any overly emotional displays. The church's organist played profoundly moving music, sending shivers through the attendees. True to tradition, the choir sang uplifting hymns about a heavenly realm of endless delights.

The entire community gathered in Indigo's backyard for the repast. They had come to celebrate Reggie's short life and long legacy. In Mississippi fashion, Cousin Mable had prepared a feast of fried chicken, collard greens, cornbread, macaroni and cheese, two kinds of punch, and peach cobbler for dessert. The tables held enough food to feed everyone, including the mailman and the insurance man. Even the local butcher, the milkman, and Mr. Nelson, who pulled his little red wagon up and down the street and begged for anything he could recycle, enjoyed equal status at the table.

The sun rested low in the sky as Cousin Mabel cleared the leftovers and removed the paper tablecloths. Seemingly from nowhere, Uncle Donny produced bottles of wine and spirits as the conversations grew louder and the stories began to flow. Indigo asked Cousin Mabel to remind everyone about the Cairo crossing so they would not forget. Cousin Mabel was a skilled storyteller.

When the Chambers family migrated to Chicago in the 1920s, Reggie's mother was just a child on a quest prompted by hope and necessity. Historians named it the Great Migration, a journey that promised to lead them away from the suffocating grip of Jim Crow's South, where despair clung to them like the thick Southern air. The Chambers forebears came on buses and trains, hearts laden with dreams and memories of a place that offered them nothing but backbreaking toil and the constant, gnawing presence of fear. They spoke of the South as a land shadowed by economic depression, where opportunities withered like crops in a drought, and hatred grew like weeds in the fertile ground of human hearts. They left that environment to find a place where they could stand beneath the sun and not feel its warmth marred by the chill of oppression. But the journey was not merely physical. It was an emotional passage from a known hell to an unknown promise. They carried with them not just their suitcases and bags but the weight of their experiences, the scars of their battles, and the fragile flame of hope.

In Cairo, Illinois, their family transitioned from Jim Crow cars to integrated ones before crossing the river to what they hoped was freedom. Reggie's family often recounted this moment, likening it to the scriptural passage from Isaiah that foretold that when they passed through the rivers, they would not drown. They whispered the passage as a mantra of faith in the face of relentless tides.

The Great Migration brought immense opportunities—economic upliftment and an escape from the blatant cruelties of Jim Crow. Yet, it also bore the seeds of new challenges: racial tensions in crowded Northern cities, substandard living conditions, and a nostalgia for the South. The move reshaped not just the lives of those who migrated but the very fabric of American society. Yet, the migration was also a trail of sacrifices. Families were split, livelihoods abandoned, and a new type of struggle was faced in the bustling anonymity of Northern metropolises. The racism was less overt, perhaps, but no less insidious, manifesting in economic disparities and segregated living conditions that mirrored the old oppressions in new guises.

###

After Reggie's funeral services, Hannah's energy was sapped. Amidst the howling winds outside, she lay restless in bed. The recent funeral and the somber repast lingered heavily in her thoughts, casting long shadows across her spirit that sleep could not dispel. As she wrestled with her blankets, Hannah visualized herself lagging behind as others had already crossed a symbolic river, moving ahead without her. She stood on the bank, hesitating, the river's current fierce and intimidating. In this moment of solitude and struggle, she thought she heard the wind's barely discernible whisper guiding her through her river of sadness. "You are not alone," the voice assured. The voice suggested it was natural to seek understanding, question the profound suffering, and look for signs of benevolence even in the deepest shadows of despair. The voice implied that this spiritual challenge, while daunting, was also an opportunity to connect deeper with the mysterious interplay of life and death. Amen and Ashe.

6

2019 **COVID-19**

During the COVID-19 pandemic, the bustling atmosphere in the ED at the level-one trauma center was tense and urgent, resembling a warzone where life, death, and all shades of human suffering converged. The influx of patients during heightened demand often threatened to overwhelm the department's capacity, creating a frantic dance of overcrowding, extended wait times, and delayed treatments. Visually, the scene in the ED was harrowing. Patients lay on stretchers, covered in blood and bandages, while doctors and nurses darted from one to another, performing life-saving procedures under harsh, bright lights that cast stark shadows on the walls. The smells of antiseptic, blood, and bodily fluids permeated the air, heavy with the scents of disinfectant and sterile gloves, mingling with the acrid stench of vomit. The pervasive odor of sickness and injury was inescapable despite rigorous cleaning efforts.

The relentless cacophony unnerved Hannah. Amidst this chaos, she observed the profound impact the lockdowns had on the emotions, stamina, and health of the medical team, including doctors, nurses, and chaplains. These professionals grappled with unprecedented challenges and pressures as they fought the virus and tended to critically ill patients. The isolation compounded their stress, anxiety, and grief, severely restricting their ability to seek comfort from friends and loved ones.

At the pandemic's peak, every room Hannah checked was filled. She methodically visited the bays, encountering cases ranging from motor vehicle accidents to respiratory distress. Tragically, three of the patients she attended to succumbed before she could complete her rounds. During one particularly distressing moment, Hannah was summoned to support the family of a sixteen-year-old boy with special needs who had coded. The examination room was too small to accommodate non-medical personnel, heightening the family's distress. The boy's grandmother, fearing exposure to the virus, regretted not acting on her instincts sooner, which might have saved her grandson. Within minutes of the doctors explaining the gravity of the situation, the boy passed away. Later, Hannah encountered a forty-eight-year-old man who had attempted suicide. In the presence of a resident and his wife in attendance, he regretted his actions and confessed his remorse to Hannah and God.

Interpersonal challenges were also common. Hannah often needed more support from her manager, Waymond, whose leadership style was authoritarian and dismissive. His demands were high, yet he provided little guidance or resources, making it challenging for her to meet his expectations or effectively fulfill her responsibilities. She also felt this need for more support from her colleagues. They, too, were burdened by their frustrations and challenges, and they seldom offered the camaraderie or assistance she desperately needed.

###

The pressure was immense, with a high workload, tight time constraints, and the complex emotional needs of patients and families. These expectations came from all directions—Hannah's manager, her peers, and, not least of all, herself. Striving to meet these demands invariably led to more stress and a dwindling sense of job satisfaction.

Day in and day out, she was confronted with illness, loss, and trauma. Witnessing such profound suffering and being there in the most heartbreaking moments of people's lives led to what she feared was the onset of compassion fatigue and burnout. This emotional exhaustion only deepened her feelings of disillusionment and frustration. Faced with these overwhelming challenges, she knew she needed to find ways to cope.

By the following Friday, Hannah was stressed out and suffering from a deep state of depression. Suddenly, she felt overwhelmed and underappreciated. The enthusiasm she had initially felt as she cared for the dying and the families of the deceased had waned, diminishing to a superficial exercise of going through the motions. To exacerbate matters, the most recent version of the upcoming schedule had her working six days in a row with no day off. She would have no time to decompress or reflect, with minimal downtime between shifts.

###

Hannah's decision to enter chaplaincy had not been made lightly. It had been a leap of faith, a surrendering to the unknown, and a departure from the academic world that measured success in publications and grants, not spiritual enlightenment. She couldn't shake off the fear that she might have made the wrong career choice, questioning whether she truly belonged in this new world of chaplaincy. Physically, the toll of chaplaincy was evident in the dark circles under her eyes, and exhaustion seeped into her bones. Her body rebelled against the relentless demands, craving rest and nourishment that seemed out of reach. She struggled to balance and prioritize self-care amid the chaos surrounding her. Spiritually, the elusive search for meaning and purpose exacerbated the emptiness that still lingered within her. As someone deeply embedded in the helping professions, Hannah understood the heavy toll that overexertion and stress could exact on those committed to caring for others. Whether they were healthcare workers, social workers, teachers, counselors, or first responders, their demands could negatively impact their professional lives and well-being. She examined the phenomenon through analytical eyes.

Firstly, there was burnout. This wasn't just about feeling tired; it was a profound sense of emotional exhaustion that seeped into every aspect of one's life. It was characterized by detachment, a sense of not making a difference anymore. And with that came a significantly decreased sense of personal accomplishment. One started to feel cynical, detached, and utterly unmotivated. It was a dangerous place to be when one's job was about connecting with and helping others.

Then, there was compassion fatigue. Imagine being constantly bombarded with the suffering and trauma of others. Over time, this exposure could lead to emotional numbness—compassion fatigue. One could not empathize as they used to; they felt numb and tired. The capacity to care, which once seemed inexhaustible, began to dwindle.

Hannah observed that physical health problems were also a significant concern. The relentless stress and the long hours didn't just wear down one's mind; they also wore down one's body. Headaches, muscle tension, insomnia, and gastrointestinal issues became frequent companions for many. Moreover, there was the looming threat of more severe conditions like heart disease and diabetes, brought on by chronic stress.

The temptation to give up had brushed against Hannah more times than she could count. Yet, surrender did not align with her intrinsic nature, inherited from her mother, a solitary warrior raising three children alone while defying unimaginable challenges. The idea of being a tenacious woman carried a certain allure, even though the reality of her daily grind held no glamor. Nevertheless, Hannah became frustrated and thought about quitting her job.

###

Hannah stopped in the hospital chapel before clocking out for the day. Nestled quietly in the corner of the chapel was a fountain. The space was filled with the gentle murmur of water cascading over stones. Hannah closed her eyes and relaxed to the sounds of the water in the background. She swayed slightly to the rhythm of the wash. She picked up a Bible and read Psalm 139, profoundly reflecting on its message. Then, she closed her eyes and prayed.

"Are you there, God?" she whispered.

"Can you hear my voice, Holy Spirit?" she questioned.

"Do you have the power to guide me, Jesus?" she prayed.

"I relinquished all I had, believing it was your call I was answering. Now, I stand at a crossroads, uncertain of my next step. I'm at a loss for what action to take. Please point me in the right direction, and I promise to follow where you lead."

###

Hannah imagined hearing a voice speaking to her. After a grueling day at the hospital, navigating the relentless challenges of the COVID-19 crisis, Hannah felt profoundly depleted. In this moment of quiet reflection, Hannah turned her thoughts to Psalm 139, a scripture that had always offered her solace and strength. The words of the Psalm reminded her that she was never truly alone; the Holy Presence was a constant companion, intimately aware of her every moment, providing comfort and guidance even in the darkest times.

God's omnipresence brought a renewed sense of hope and strength. As she delved deeper into the themes of the Psalm—unconditional love, divine guidance, and sovereignty—Hannah felt herself drawing closer to God's heart, intimately involved in every detail of her life. She was reminded that she was made with wonder, affirming her inherent value and God's intentional artistry in her creation. This was a profound comfort in a world that often questioned her worth and challenged her purpose. The psalm laid a foundation for Hannah's hope and perseverance, providing comfort, strength, and reassurance regardless of her uncertainties and difficulties. It encouraged her to trust, to surrender her fears and doubts, and to rest in the assurance of God's unfailing love. Amen and Ashe.

7

2020 **George Floyd**

On May 25, 2020, in Minneapolis, Minnesota, a deeply troubling event unfolded that underscored the persistent issues of police brutality and systemic racism in the United States. George Floyd, a forty-six-year-old Black man, met a grim fate at the hands of Derek Chauvin, a White police officer. Captured on video, Floyd's final moments were harrowing. Floyd lay pinned to the ground, Chauvin's knee suffocatingly pressed against his neck, gasping for air and pleading for his life. The footage sparked a global outcry—a visceral reaction to the utter disregard for Floyd's humanity and the stark cruelty of Chauvin's actions. It was a raw manifestation of the racism and abuse of power that had seeped deep into the criminal justice system. Citizens who saw the video began to realize that within the ranks of law enforcement lurked a faction bereft of compassion and empathy in its approach to policing. To them, their job was not about protecting and serving the community but rather about asserting their authority and keeping what they perceived as the "bad elements" of society in check.

Carrying with them personal prejudices and racial biases, these officers viewed specific individuals, particularly those from marginalized communities, with disdain and suspicion. When encountering lawbreakers, these officers did not hesitate to use brutal force to constrain them, resorting to violence and aggression as their primary means of control. A lack of remorse or compassion marked their actions, as they viewed those they deemed as criminals as deserving of harsh treatment. The abuse of power and disregard for human dignity that characterized their actions only deepened the divide between law enforcement and the people they were meant to protect. Despite calls for accountability and reform, this faction within law enforcement remained entrenched in its beliefs and practices. The consequences of their actions reverberated throughout the community, leaving a trail of pain and mistrust in their wake. It was within this climate that George Floyd's death occurred. The social mood surrounding the murder of George Floyd was one of deep-seated tension, frustration, and anger.

In the days following Floyd's murder, outrage permeated the streets of Minneapolis and swiftly spread across cities nationwide and around the world. Protesters, driven by a collective fury and exasperation, demanded justice for Floyd and called for an end to the systemic racism and police brutality that disproportionately affected people of color. The streets echoed with calls for accountability, urging a complete overhaul of law enforcement practices.

Yet, as these peaceful protests grew, a darker narrative emerged. Some criminally minded citizens saw the unrest as an opportunity to further their agendas. Masked as allies, these infiltrators and agitators hijacked the genuine calls for justice, inciting violence and chaos. They looted, vandalized, and set fires, marring the protest's intent and causing harm to communities already in distress from Floyd's tragic death. Law enforcement officers and community leaders scrambled to weed out these disruptive forces, striving to preserve the sanctity of the protests while safeguarding the rights and safety of all involved.

George Floyd's death and the subsequent outcry became a potent reminder of the deep-seated inequalities still rampant in society. It galvanized a movement for racial justice and equality, pushing for significant reforms in policing and a broad reckoning with the ingrained racism that permeated every aspect of American life. The overwhelming solidarity in the face of such adversity underscored the public's demand for a society that truly respects the dignity and humanity of all its members.

###

The emergence of a movement to raise voices and signs against injustice was swift and resolute. It included passionate Black Lives Matter advocates, prophetic pastors, and individuals like Hannah, who had reached their breaking point with society's pervasive injustices—this diverse coalition of voices united in a shared mission for change. Protests erupted in cities and towns across the country, drawing crowds of impassioned demonstrators who marched with signs bearing messages of solidarity, demands for justice, and calls to end police brutality. The movement transcended boundaries of race, ethnicity, and socioeconomic status as people of all backgrounds joined together in a collective cry for accountability and reform. Among the protesters were grieving mothers who had lost sons and daughters to senseless acts of violence, their voices echoing with pain and resilience as they demanded justice for their loved ones.

Women like Hannah, who had grown tired of witnessing the unchecked injustices, found their voices amplified in the chorus of protest. Their presence and determination added a powerful dimension to the movement, highlighting the urgency and importance of confronting systemic racism and police brutality. Their protests symbolized unity and defiance, a testament to the strength and resilience of a community united in its resolve to stand up against injustice. Through its collective action and unwavering commitment, the people's voices rang out loud and clear, demanding a more just and equitable society.

###

As the COVID-19 lockdowns were lifted and people began to emerge from their homes, a darker side of society also began to reveal itself. With the streets once again becoming populated, looters, muggers, and other lawbreakers saw an opportunity to prey on innocent people and sow chaos. They lurked in the shadows, waiting for the right moment to strike. Stores that had just reopened found themselves targets of looting, with thieves taking advantage of the chaos to steal whatever they could get their hands on. The once bustling streets now felt dangerous and threatening, with the presence of these criminals casting a dark shadow over the city.

Dedicated members of the police force who had been working long hours without respite pushed themselves to their limits. The constant threat of violence and the ever-present danger lurking in the streets added to their anxiety. These officers, already stretched thin from the demands of enforcing lockdown measures, found themselves even more overworked and under immense pressure. As the first responders to the chaos unfolding in the city, the officers were constantly alert. The stress of the situation weighed heavily on their shoulders as they worked to maintain order and ensure the community's safety.

Hannah still worked in the hospital as a PRN to earn income and make ends meet. Because she was not full-time, her assignments typically involved the busy trauma units of the ED. One night, accompanied by two dozen police officers, Juliette Coleman arrived in the trauma unit with a gunshot wound to her head. She died a short time later, the victim of suicide.

This thirty-two-year-old Black female, Officer Juliette Coleman, had served on the force for five years, answering what she considered a call to "protect and serve." During her early days on the force, before the riots, Juliette had been involved with many of the community policing initiatives like "coffee with a cop" and CAPS. All of that came to a halt with the pandemic-related lootings, the police-involved killing of George Floyd, and calls for defunding of the police departments. In the wake of escalated violence and negative media portrayals of law enforcement, some officers like Juliette Coleman suffered from trauma and depression. Officer Coleman saw suicide as the only way out. During a press conference following Officer Coleman's death, the spokesperson noted that suicide among police officers had increased. The officer's mother and father were inconsolable when they arrived in the ED. Hannah did everything she could to provide support and spiritual care to the grieving family.

###

Sitting at a quaint outdoor table, Hannah and Indigo relished the simple pleasure of dining al fresco after months confined indoors due to COVID-19 restrictions. Around them, the world seemed cautiously awakening, mirroring their sense of renewal. The air was fragrant with the scent of spring blossoms and freshly mown grass, each breath a reminder of the seasons cycling forward despite the challenges faced.

They each sipped iced tea, the clink of ice against glass punctuating their conversation, and shared a salad bursting with the colors of newly ripened vegetables. A gentle breeze, warm and inviting, wove through the scene, carrying with it the distant sounds of the city slowly coming back to life. This simple meal outdoors was a small reclaiming of freedom, a moment of peace and pleasure amid a world that had changed. It was a poignant reminder of life's enduring tenacity amidst uncertain times for Hannah and Indigo.

"Indigo, every time I turn on the news, it's like a punch to the gut. What's happening in Lewis Town—the growing divide—is heartbreaking. We've got to do something; we can't just sit back and watch."

"I know, Hannah, it's infuriating. Every day in the classroom, I see the effects of these racial tensions firsthand. We need a plan that tackles the problem from all angles. We've got to address the biases, educate everyone about systemic racism, and start breaking down these barriers that keep perpetuating inequality."

"Exactly! And it's not just about the present, either. We have to look at the historical injustices that have led us here. If we're going to heal as a community, we have to acknowledge our shared history and work towards genuine reconciliation."

"We have an upcoming meeting of the Lewis Town City Council, right? We should use that opportunity to push for real, open conversations about race. It's about time we challenged our biases, listened to each other, and learned from each other."

"I agree. And it's not just about talking—we need action. We can't underestimate the power of advocacy and activism. We have to amplify the marginalized voices and push for policies that bring about equity. Education, healthcare, and employment are all areas where systemic inequalities must be addressed head-on."

"Partnerships are going to be key, Hannah. We should work with local organizations, schools, businesses—anyone committed to making a difference. It's about building a coalition that can impact our community."

"It's going to be tough, no doubt. But it's necessary. We've got to stand up and be the allies we claim to be. It's time to take to the streets to make our voices heard. Lewis Town needs us to fight for what's right."

"Let's get everyone at the meeting to commit to something actionable. It's not just about feeling frustrated—it's about turning that frustration into something positive that can make a difference."

"I'm with you, Indigo. Let's do this. Let's turn our anger and frustration into a force for good—for justice, for equality, for Lewis Town."

###

On her screened-in porch, Hannah sat pensively, reflecting on the tumultuous events of the past Saturday. It had been a day marked by the disruption that cast a long shadow over her small community's quest for justice and peace. The protest that day was supposed to be a peaceful demonstration, a collective call for long overdue reforms. However, as Hannah thought back, her heart sank with the realization of how quickly the actions of a few had overshadowed their pure intentions. These individuals, seemingly indifferent to the cause, had infiltrated the protest, their recklessness fueling a narrative that neither represented the community's spirit nor its demands.

As the night deepened and the light on her porch flickered gently, Hannah noted the concerns she would present at the next City Council meeting. In this quiet moment of reflection, Hannah felt a renewed sense of commitment to her community. It was a commitment to understand, empathize, and act. As the evening gave way to night, she knew the journey ahead would be long and fraught with challenges, but it was a journey she was ready to take for the sake of all who called this place home. Amen and Ashe.

8

2021 **Nadia's Story**

A call came over the intercom: "PEDS Chaplain to NICU, STAT." Hannah rushed to answer because the matter sounded urgent. When she arrived, the nurse filled her in. The patient was a seventeen-year-old young woman whose infant was critically ill. Hannah's pastoral instincts alerted her to be a comforting presence and an empathetic listener. Her motherly instincts signaled her heart to console this young woman whose baby was about to die. At the same time, her cultural instincts told her that this young mother was well-acquainted with death and grief. Her ultimate goal was to be a nonjudgmental, supportive presence.

"Hi, Nadia. My name is Hannah. I'm one of the chaplains here at the hospital. Would it be okay if I kept you company until your parents arrive?"

The young mother made a slight moaning noise, which Hannah took as consent. Nadia was sitting in a rocking chair; she appeared sad and troubled. She wore hospital pajamas and a bonnet to keep her hair pulled back. She rocked back and forth to the rhythmic whisper of the life support systems that were keeping her baby alive.

The room had bright lights, and the chilliness made Hannah tightly wrap her sweater around her body.

"Yes. It's okay." Nadia answered.

As Hannah pulled a chair beside her, Nadia began to cry softly. It was as if she suddenly permitted her tears to flow. She wiped her eyes with the tissue Hannah handed her.

They sat in silence for a few minutes. Hannah's eyes finally rested on the incubator in the middle of the room. It held a disfigured infant still covered with traces of blood, mucous, and other fluids. The child was tiny–barely large enough to fill both palms cupped together. Tubes hung from her nasal passages. A small hospital bracelet showed the baby's gender and the mother's name. Hannah began to speak quietly when she saw that Nadia's tears had subsided somewhat.

"What's going on, Nadia?"

Nadia cleared her throat. "My baby is sick. They keep telling me I need to let them remove the tubes. But I don't want to do that. I'm not ready to do that yet."

"I'm listening. Go on," Hannah said as she leaned toward her slightly to close the distance between them.

"It's so much. Too much. I didn't even know I was pregnant. She was born three days ago. Now, my little girl is hanging on. She's so tiny. I was recovering upstairs when they told me I needed to come here quickly. They said my baby's oxygen was dropping, and her heart rate was slowing down. They keep telling me I need to let them remove the tubes. They keep pressuring me. But no. I don't want to do that. I'm not ready to do that." She said, shaking her head back and forth to signal her disagreement with the team's suggestion.

Hannah lowered her voice to a soothing whisper.

"It's a tough decision. But you are the only one who can make it." They sat in silence for a few minutes. "How are you feeling about all this?"

"I don't know. My feelings are everywhere: sad, scared, frustrated, everything."

"I can see a lot is going on. How can I support you?"

"I don't know. I don't know."

Nadia turned her gaze toward her baby. Nadia's expression changed to one of troubled tenderness mixed with confusion. They sat silently as she rocked back and forth and observed her daughter breathing in and out. After a few minutes, Nadia began to speak again.

"She's so small. She weighed less than two pounds when she was born. They said they might have to do chest compressions if her heart stopped.

But look at her. That would hurt her little chest and break her skin because she's so fragile. Her skin would tear."

Nadia wiped her eyes. She continued to rock as if the motion would help her think better. Nadia looked at the heart rate monitor.

"Look," she pointed to the monitor. "Her heart rate is going up. It was in the thirties. Now it's in the forties. She's a fighter. I want to let her keep on fighting."

"I can see that. What did the doctors tell you?"

"They said she would probably not live very long. I know that. But I'm not ready to have them remove the tubes. I want to give her a chance to fight. I want to leave it in God's hands." Nadia explained.

"It sounds like you're a woman of faith. How is your faith speaking to you right now?" Hannah asked.

"Yeah, I have faith. I don't go to church much, but I believe in God. And I pray. My decision doesn't matter; I believe God will have the last say," Nadia replied.

Nadia continued to rock in her chair. Hannah let silence take the lead in the conversation, wanting to empower Nadia and not burden her with guilt over the impending loss of her baby. After a long time of silence, Nadia reopened the conversation.

"I have a one-year-old son at home," Nadia said, slightly laughing. "He's a handful. He doesn't walk yet but scoots along on his bottom and climbs. I found him in my closet one day." Nadia chuckled. "He's very curious."

Nadia rocked in silence for a few minutes.

"After graduation, I got a job at a big box store." She described her job as a retail clerk. "I'm quitting in the fall to go back to school. My high school counselor helped me apply for a nursing school scholarship. I begin classes in the fall."

"Congratulations. That's good news."

"Yeah, I like that science stuff. I believe I can make a difference. I'll be able to get a decent job when I finish the nursing program. Maybe I can work at this hospital. Then, I can take care of my son. My grandmother thinks I'll make a fine nurse.

There was a comfortable silence.

"I love my grandmother. I've lived with her since I was a little girl. She raised me. I help take care of her at home. I would do anything for her."

Nadia's spirit seemed to lift a bit. It was encouraging that she was ready to move past this tragedy to pursue her future. She was determined to muster her inner strength and achieve her goals. She was ready to fight the odds that were stacked against her. Her faith in God contributed to her determination to succeed. Hannah could see it in Nadia's eyes when she talked about her son. This young woman wanted to give her remaining child (the one-year-old) the best life possible.

At that moment, the nurse walked in.

"Nadia, your grandmother is on the telephone. I told her you would call her back."

Nadia returned her grandmother's call on her cell phone. The tone of her voice and expression showed that her spirit had lifted a bit.

"What advice did your grandmother have for you?" Hannah asked after Nadia hung up the phone.

"She told me I should be firm and pray about it. And then leave it in God's hands."

Throughout her encounter, Nadia let her faith influence her choices. She was already grieving the loss of her daughter, so she had a chance to start processing the finality of it all. At the same time, she found peace in leaving the outcome of her daughter's situation in God's hands.

"Sounds like good advice. Would you like me to pray for you now or later?" Hannah asked.

"Later, maybe."

"Okay. I will pray for you when I talk to God later tonight. Is that okay?" Hannah asked.

Nadia nodded in agreement.

"I'm going to pray, too," Nadia said. "And then, I'm going to leave it in God's hands."

There was a knock on the door. Nadia's mother and father had arrived. The nurse left the room to give them some privacy. After about ten minutes, the doctor signaled that the team was ready to give the family a medical update and asked everyone to join them in the room. The doctor clarified to Nadia that the baby's condition was not likely to improve.

"When the baby's oxygen and heart rate drop again, the medical team needs to know what action to take. We need to know if you want us to attempt to revive the child."

Then, the doctor described a second option.

"If you decide the team should not give the baby chest compressions or take other active steps to revive your baby, you can just hold your child in your arms and comfort her until she slips away."

Oblivious to what was occurring in the room, Nadia's eyes were fixed on her baby throughout the explanations. Nadia's parents asked the team a few clarifying questions while Nadia continued to focus on her child in the incubator. Nadia finally made her decision, saying that she would like to hold her baby until she slipped away if her heart stopped again. Nadia's parents supported her decision. After that, the medical team left the room. Hannah went to the chapel for a moment of quiet.

To this point, Nadia's life had been a series of trials and tribulations, but she remained resilient and determined to create a better future for herself and her son. Her faith and inner strength were the guiding lights that carried her through the darkest moments. She had faced the loss of her baby with grace and courage, finding solace in the belief that everything happened for a reason. As she prepared to start her nursing program, Nadia was hopeful and determined. She saw this opportunity as a chance to make a difference in the world and use her science talents to help others in need. Her grandmother's encouragement and support echoed in her mind, fueling her ambition to succeed.

###

Another turbulent Saturday unfolded as the community grappled with the ongoing tensions. Protests became magnets for various causes, with a diverse mix of participants who converged in the plaza. The day began with the usual enthusiasm—chants filled the air, signs waved, and the atmosphere was charged with protesters' determination and the watchful eyes of law enforcement. But the dynamics shifted dramatically when external agitators, some intent on wreaking havoc, infiltrated the ranks of genuine demonstrators.

The situation escalated when an eighteen-wheeler, driven with deliberate recklessness, plowed through an intersection crowded with protesters. Ignoring the red light, the truck driver aimed his vehicle to strike pedestrians in the crosswalk and collided with an SUV, causing widespread destruction and panic. The crash brought down the honorary street sign at the intersection of Jordan Avenue and Independence Boulevard, adding to the chaos and halting traffic in every direction. Emergency services responded swiftly, their sirens piercing the confusion as they rushed the injured to Southwest Memorial Hospital. The severity of the incident was broadcast live, with news reporters at the scene detailing the tragic toll: at least eighteen injuries and one fatality.

###

A special report interrupted the regularly scheduled program as the TV anchor related the story.

"Good evening. We begin tonight with a heart-wrenching story from our community. Nadia Collins, a dedicated nursing student whose aspirations to heal and help others were well known, met with a tragic accident that left the city in shock.

"On her way to class, in what can only be described as a harrowing twist of fate, Nadia was fatally injured. An angry truck driver plowed through the intersection, striking several pedestrians in the crosswalk. A street sign, knocked down by the rampaging vehicle, fell and struck Collins, a nursing student on her way to class, eager to continue her studies. Reports indicate the vehicle deliberately careened into the crowd. The ensuing chaos led to Nadia being hit by the dislodged street sign, a devastating blow that would ultimately claim her life. The truck driver is in custody tonight.

"The loss of Nadia has deeply affected not only her family, who are understandably devastated but also a community that knew her as a bright light, full of potential and compassion. Our thoughts are with Nadia's loved ones during this tough time. Joanne Barnes, Network News Anchor."

The broadcast of Nadia's death spread quickly, sending shockwaves through the neighborhood. People were outraged at the senseless loss of such a promising young life. The crowd refused to let her death be in vain. Nadia's memory became a rallying cry for a community united in their outrage. They took to the streets, demanding justice for Nadia and calling for accountability. They held vigils, lit candles, and shared stories of Nadia's kindness and determination. Her death catalyzed change, inspiring others to speak out and demand accountability for injustice in its multifaceted guises.

###

Hannah silently gazed through the screens of her porch, overwhelmed by the weight of sorrow for Nadia, whose life had been cut short. Nadia had become an innocent victim in the relentless struggle for justice and peace. Hannah remembered their first encounter in the emergency department of the hospital, where Nadia was bracing herself for the imminent loss of her daughter. Despite such profound grief, Nadia clung to the dream of becoming a nurse to support her surviving son. She was determined to learn everything necessary to care for him, setting off to her classes daily, filled with hope and commitment.

Nadia's abrupt death sent shockwaves through the community, leaving everyone to grapple with the lost potential of a woman who could have healed many. As the community grieved, so did Hannah, feeling the encroaching darkness and silence around her. The stark reality hit her: life was incredibly fragile. In her heart, Hannah offered a prayer for compassion and mercy upon the people and the world. "Have mercy on your people and your world," she prayed. "Amen and Ashe."

9

2021 **Calvin's Story**

Calvin had always been a sensitive soul, finely attuned to the emotions of those around him, most notably his mother, Hannah. From a young age, he displayed an uncanny ability to read her moods and needs. If Hannah felt sorrow, Calvin was there with a comforting hug or a gentle smile, eager to alleviate her sadness. When frustration furrowed her brow, he would lighten the mood with a joke, a melody on the piano, or a silly dance, all to dispel her discontent. His connection with his mother was profound and mutual; the bond she shared with Calvin, her only son among her children, was intense, echoing a heritage of familial bonds.

As Calvin entered his teenage years, his aspirations began to crystallize around a future in music. While he regarded academics as a means to an end, his passion was rooted in the rhythms and harmonies that spoke to his soul. Hannah supported his musical ambitions wholeheartedly, providing him with cultural experiences that extended well beyond their immediate environment, aiming to broaden his horizons.

However, as he entered adolescence, Calvin became increasingly aware of the harsh realities of discrimination. The prevailing segregation and exclusion cast a shadow over his days. Protective as ever, Hannah endeavored to shield her son from these brutal truths, always prioritizing his emotional health. Regardless of the societal challenges, Calvin remained focused. He had no interest in social justice marches or competitive academic pursuits but in creating and sharing beautiful music that could comfort and perhaps even transform the world.

Calvin was on his way to band practice on the day of the latest unrest. The air was tense as opposing groups clashed during the protest. The protests had no rhyme or rhythm; the scene was chaotic, with advocates from different causes. Typically, Calvin would have steered clear of such turmoil, but something compelled him to move forward on this day.

As he neared the intersection, the atmosphere thickened; voices raised in anger, and the confrontation escalated. Suddenly, amidst the chaos, a gun was drawn, and a shot fired. A stray bullet, intended for no specific target yet endangering everyone, struck Calvin. In that tragic moment, a life brimming with potential and dreams of musical artistry was cut devastatingly short. The community was left to mourn the loss of a young musician—a tender soul determined to heal the world with his art, now silenced far too soon.

###

Hannah's world came to a halt when the devastating news of Calvin's death reached her. The tragic and senseless murder of her only son, struck down by a stray bullet during a protest, plunged her into profound grief and despair. It felt like a vital part of her existence had been abruptly and cruelly severed. Her heart was burdened with the weight of an irreplaceable loss.

In the wake of Calvin's death, Hannah's perception of the future was initially shrouded in darkness. The world appeared bleak, stripped of its color and warmth. Yet, despite the overwhelming shadow of her grief, her anger responded with a resilient flame of determination that began to flicker within her. She recognized that while she could never restore Calvin's life, she held the power to influence the lives of others who were navigating the same turbulent waters of sorrow.

Resolved not to let Calvin's death be in vain, Hannah committed herself to walking alongside other mothers who had faced similar tragedies. She vowed to become a pillar of support, a shoulder to lean on, and a listener to the stories of loss that echoed her own. Hannah longed to look beyond this moment of deep sadness toward a broader horizon where the relentless cycle of violence would claim no more lives. She longed to engage in community activism, participate in forums, and collaborate with organizations fighting against gun violence. Hannah desired to stem the flow of senseless killings and prevent other families from experiencing the same depths of despair. She hoped to find purpose through these connections, channeling her pain into a force for communal healing and advocacy. However, all she could accomplish at this moment was sobbing deeply over the loss of her son.

###

The ensuing days were marked by doubt and exhaustion, but she was determined to press forward. Hannah envisioned a future where communities could thrive without fearing random violence. In this future, the deep rivers of sorrow would no longer have the power to drown the hope and potential of an entire race. She carried Calvin's memory with each step forward, transforming her tragedy into a beacon of hope and change.

The pain was a sharp, suffocating ache that gripped her heart. Calvin was her joy, hope, and the pride of her life. The dreams she had nurtured for him, the future she had envisioned, were all extinguished in a moment of senseless violence. The knowledge that he had died as collateral damage during a protest—a young, vibrant life cut short on his way to pursue his passion for music—was a bitter pill that Hannah could hardly swallow.

A deep, unyielding sorrow enveloped Hannah as the days turned into weeks. The silence of his absence echoed through the house, filling each corner with memories that brought unbearable pain. Each note of music she heard was a reminder of Calvin's laughter, his excitement about a new piece he was learning, or his dreams of college and a music career.

Anger and frustration soon intertwined with her sorrow. Calvin had not been a direct participant in the protests; he had been in the wrong place at the wrong time. The thought that her son's life had been taken by the very chaos he had tried to avoid was infuriating. The pursuit of justice seemed daunting and exhausting, yet she knew she owed it to Calvin to fight for accountability and change. Haunted by what-ifs, Hannah struggled with guilt and despair. Could she have done something to protect him? What if he had taken a different route? The questions plagued her, tormenting her restless nights.

Through it all, Hannah clung to her faith and the community that rallied around her, finding solace in their shared memories of Calvin, the music he loved, and the hope that his death would not be in vain. Yet, the void left by his absence remained vast and unfillable, a constant reminder of a precious life lost and the profound changes needed to prevent such tragedies in the future.

###

As the storm brewed over the city, the dark clouds gathering ominously, Hannah stared out the window, lost in a storm of her own. The rumble of thunder seemed to echo the turmoil within her, each crash a stark reminder of the night she received the devastating news. Hannah's grief was deep and unyielding. It enveloped her, making it hard to breathe, hard to think, hard to understand how such a tragedy could have happened to her son, her joy, her pride. The randomness of his death, the cruel and abrupt snatching away of his vibrant future, seemed as unfathomable as the swirling chaos outside her window. Each day, she tried to make sense of the senseless. How could her son, who had dodged the rougher paths of life, had been filled with dreams and laughter, and had planned to fill the world with music, be gone? The injustice of it, the brutal finality, was overwhelming.

The storm outside mirrored the one within her—a mother's heart shattered by loss, struggling to comprehend the incomprehensible. Her grief was a storm, filled with moments of piercing clarity followed by darkness and confusion. The questions haunted her, relentless and unanswerable. Why Calvin? Why so young? Why by such a violent, arbitrary hand? Where was God in all of this?

As all storms do, the storm passed, leaving a silence almost as hard to bear as the noise. The world had moved on, but for her, time seemed to stand still, each tick of the clock a reminder of what could have been, of what was lost. Through it all, Hannah held onto a fragile hope that someday, somehow, she might find meaning in this tragedy, a way to channel her grief into something that could prevent another storm like the one that took Calvin. Until then, she would endure her sorrow as deep as the river, her spirit as restless as the stormy winds, her heart forever echoing with the refrain of what was and what could never be again. Amen and Ashe.

10

2021 **A Matter of Life**

Indigo sat at Hannah's kitchen table. It was rare for them to get together on a Saturday morning. Their hands were occupied with busyness to keep their minds from dwelling on the tragedies that had touched them both. Hannah brought pound cake and coffee to the table and set it before her friend.

"Tell me what you think of that pound cake. It was my mother's recipe." Hannah served a slice of the famous cake on her grandmother's China dessert plates. She even brought out the cloth napkins for the occasion.

"Mmmm, so good!" was all Indigo could say as she let the buttery treat melt in her mouth.

Hannah smiled. "I'm glad you like it. I used my standing mixer to whip the butter and sugar until it was fluffy. Then, I added the dry ingredients a little at a time. I think that's the trick to making the cake moist."

"Well, whatever you did, this is delicious." Indigo's eyes rested on the television screen. A newscaster was reporting on the latest riots involving Black Lives Matter. "There's another rally going on. Every day, there seems to be more unrest."

As the women watched the TV coverage, it was hard to tell what the rally was about. The diversity of the banners and placards was striking. Each sign represented a different facet of the nation's ideological divide. The spectrum ranged from "Black Lives Matter" to "Blue Lives Matter" and from calls to "End Police Brutality" to demands to "End Racism Now." Some signs supported "Trump 2000," declared "Hands Up, Don't Shoot," denounced "Leftist Terrorists," and even some displayed Nazi swastikas and Confederate flags. The scene was a vivid tableau of the country's deep-seated ideological rifts.

"I know," Hannah replied. "For me, the jury is still out on Black Lives Matter. Lately, I've been weighing the positives and negatives."

"I know what you mean," Indigo replied. "Some people say the group is too radical and divisive."

"The organization has been accused of instigating the looting and violence that occurs during some protests. Many critics say the organization attracts unscrupulous imposters who seize the moment to voice grievances that have nothing to do with the social activism focus of BLM."

In her curiosity, Hannah had delved into the origins and impacts of the Black Lives Matter movement. She learned that the movement began in 2013, initiated by three visionary Black women as a reaction to the acquittal of George Zimmerman after the tragic shooting of Trayvon Martin. The organization spread its message through social media using the hashtag #BlackLivesMatter; it rapidly expanded into a national and global demand for change.

Indigo still needed to be convinced. "As Black women, do you think our notions about justice align with those of Black Lives Matter?"

"I'm starting to think so," Hannah mused. "We both believe in equality and standing up for those who are marginalized and oppressed."

Hannah recalled the increased visibility and momentum of the movement following the devastating deaths of Michael Brown in Ferguson in 2014 and George Floyd in Minneapolis in 2020. Both incidents involved Black, unarmed men who died at the hands of police, triggering worldwide protests and calls for justice. The movement not only sought justice for those who were lost but also accountability for the officers involved and aimed to address the underlying racial inequalities.

"Through protests, advocacy, and grassroots organizing, the Black Lives Matter movement persistently raised awareness of issues like police violence, racial profiling, and systemic racism within the criminal justice system," Hannah responded.

"I guess there is value in how they are raising the level of awareness about some people's attitudes towards Black lives and social justice." Indigo reflected. "As far as Black women are concerned, the whole issue of social justice is complicated by how race, gender, and class shape our experiences of oppression and liberation."

Hannah reflected on Indigo's words. Emphasizing what occurs at the intersection of these three constructs was central to the Black Lives Matter ethos and Black women's ways of acquiring knowledge and justifying the truth of what they know. For Black women, their wisdom includes book knowledge but also encompasses consciousness from the legacy of slavery and beyond. Their wisdom flows not only from what their minds have read but also from what their bodies have endured and their souls have remembered. Both BLM and Black women share a collective pain and a resolve to challenge oppressive systems and amplify marginalized voices.

After studying the issues, Hannah understood that the Black Lives Matter movement, like any extensive organization, was a complex entity with commendable and questionable elements within its ranks. BLM and Black women also had their differences. Black women generally center on the experiences and perspectives of intersectionality within the context of Christianity. On the other hand, Black Lives Matter comprises a social movement focused on addressing systemic racism and police violence, not necessarily grounded in religious or theological frameworks. Many Black women embrace spirituality and religious practices, while Black Lives Matter prioritizes social and political activism.

Overall, however, Black Lives Matter adherents and Black women in general shared a commitment to challenging systems of oppression and centering the voices and experiences of Black people at the margins. Not only that, but Black Lives Matter was also adept at organizing effective rallies and marshaling resources for their cause.

Hannah set down her empty coffee cup and turned to Indigo. "I think we might have some things to learn from BLM."

###

Despite the movement's complexity and often contentious reputation, BLM had demonstrated its capability to organize impactful events. Hannah saw them as seasoned experts from whom she could learn valuable insights about event organization. She hoped to harness this knowledge for her causes. Motivated to effect change, she took the bold step of approaching Black Lives Matter representatives. Her conversation with Freddie and

Stephanie was full of informative points. The BLM leaders did most of the talking while Hannah listened and took notes.

"Hey Hannah, Freddie greeted her with a big and cheerful voice. Stephanie and I are happy to help in any way we can. It would be best to remember that one of the most important things to do when organizing a protest rally is to build a strong coalition. Make sure to reach out to other community organizations, activists, and allies to build a diverse and inclusive group of supporters. Collaboration and solidarity are key in making the event successful."

Stephanie leaned forward, nodding in agreement with what Freddie said.

"It is also crucial to plan strategically. Hannah, it would be best to start by developing a clear and achievable goal for the protest rally and a detailed logistics, communication, and safety plan. Setting a timeline, securing necessary permits, and coordinating with local law enforcement are essential to ensure a well-organized and safe event."

"It's important to center the voices and experiences of marginalized individuals, especially Black women, LGBTQ+ individuals, and other marginalized groups, in the planning and execution of the protest rally. Including others will ensure that the rally is inclusive and representative of the community it aims to serve." Freddie continued.

"Let's not overlook the importance of practicing nonviolent resistance," Stephanie added. "Peaceful and nonviolent protest tactics are vital in advancing the rally's goals. Black Lives Matter leaders advocate for nonviolent resistance to challenge injustice and create meaningful change while ensuring the safety and well-being of participants."

"Thanks!" Hannah chimed in. "These are great insights. What cautions and drawbacks should I consider when organizing a protest rally?"

Freddie responded: "Well, one potential challenge to consider is the potential for counter-protests or backlash from individuals or groups who may oppose the message or goals of the protest rally. Have a safety plan and remain vigilant during the event."

"You also have to be sure to familiarize yourself with local laws and regulations regarding protest rallies, permits, and public demonstrations," Stephanie said. "Violating laws or ordinances can have legal consequences and may jeopardize the event's success."

"What about media coverage?" Hannah asked. "How should I navigate that aspect?"

"Good question," Freddie replied. "Be prepared for media coverage and scrutiny of the protest rally. It's important to have a communications plan in place to effectively convey the message and goals of the event to the public and media outlets."

Hannah summarized in her notes: "Overall, then, organizing a successful protest rally requires careful planning, strategic coordination, and a commitment to nonviolent resistance and inclusive activism. By following these guidelines and being aware of potential challenges and drawbacks, I'll have a better chance of ensuring the rally is impactful, safe, and effective in advancing the cause of racial justice and equality."

"You got it!" Stephanie replied.

###

Having begun to organize the rally, Hannah quickly realized she needed money to carry out her vision. Determined, she plunged into the digital world, seeking advice from experienced organizers within the Black Lives Matter movement on how to fund such events.

During her online exploration, Hannah stumbled upon several fundraising strategies endorsed by these seasoned activists. The first piece of advice she found was to kick off a crowdfunding campaign using platforms like GoFundMe or Kickstarter. By tapping into her network, reaching out to the community, and rallying allies, she could effectively spread the word and drum up support for the cause.

The next tip suggested forging partnerships with local businesses, community organizations, and advocacy groups that resonated with the rally's mission and values. Such collaborations could open doors to financial support and additional resources, crucial for the rally's success.

Hannah also discovered the potential of organizing fundraising events. Ideas ranged from bake sales and benefit concerts to virtual gatherings, each providing a unique way to engage with supporters and donors and build community and solidarity around the cause.

Another avenue she explored was applying for grants. Many foundations, organizations, and institutions were keen on supporting social justice and activism initiatives, particularly those that championed grassroots movements and community-led efforts for racial justice and equality.

Lastly, she learned about the benefits of creating and selling merchandise like T-shirts, buttons, or stickers featuring messages or artwork relevant to the rally. This approach would help raise funds and enhance the cause's visibility.

With these insights, Hannah enthusiastically pursued various funding avenues. Her goal was clear: to gather the necessary financial resources to ensure the rally's success and advance the cause of racial justice and equality.

###

On a bright and sunny day, with pleasant weather conditions setting the stage for a momentous occasion, Hannah successfully orchestrated a rally to speak out against the senseless murders of young Black men and women and the brutality of the police. The participants had been informed to gather at the intersection of Jordan Avenue and Independence Boulevard, the very place where Nadia and Calvin had tragically lost their lives. Carrying signs bearing messages calling for a change in the systems of oppression, the group chanted "Justice for Nadia" and "Justice for Calvin" as they began their march.

The rally drew a diverse crowd, with at least 150 people joining to march in solidarity. They embarked on a three-mile route from the South to the North, symbolically commemorating the journey from the harsh and brutal realities of the South to the promises of freedom and equality in the North. Along the way, the participants raised their voices in unity, demanding justice and accountability for the lives lost to violence and discrimination.

As the march progressed, hecklers gathered on the sidelines, some offering encouragement while others jeered and heckled the marchers. Despite the challenges and opposition, the group remained steadfast in its commitment to raising awareness and advocating for change. To ensure the safety of all involved, police officers were in force, monitoring the rally and ensuring no injuries occurred. Their presence, although necessary, served as a reminder of the ongoing tensions and risks associated with speaking out against systemic injustices.

Hannah had thoroughly planned the rally and the subsequent program celebrating the occasion. She arranged with the City Council to culminate the march at Riverfront Park. Hannah raised enough money through donations and bake sales to purchase a park bench the city installed on the riverfront. To the bench, a tasteful plaque was attached with the names of those who had lost their lives to the violence. Indigo had arranged for an artisan to carve an equation on the back of the wooden bench. Freedom = Action + Peace + Love + Justice + e (the error term). Hannah also arranged for the city to plant an oak tree beside the bench. In the years to come, the tree's thirsty roots would grow deep and extend their reach toward the life-giving waters. Students from the local high school delivered speeches about change and equity. The protesters sang freedom songs as they released eco-friendly balloons into the atmosphere.

###

A week later, Hannah stood at the turbulent river's edge, watching the violent currents swirl under the darkening sky as a storm began to brew, mirroring her people's tumultuous history of struggle and perseverance. The once calm surface of the river now roiled with fierce currents and rising waves, a stark reminder of the dangerous and unpredictable forces at play. Despite the storm's intensity, Hannah's demeanor remained defiant and triumphant. As she observed the river's raging currents, Hannah knew now was not the time to lose balance while crossing these turbulent waters. The protest scene resonated deeply with her, evoking thoughts of historical resilience and faith, particularly of Black women who had navigated their storms throughout history.

As the storm intensified, lightning streaking across the sky and thunder echoing like war drums, Hannah thought about the daughters of Zion in biblical texts. Through unwavering faith and trust, they clung to the promise of God's everlasting covenant, reshaping their world and finding hope in their faith. Hannah felt the power of those beliefs in the howling wind and relentless rain. They were encompassed in protection that had guided the enslaved, supported the weary in exile, and healed the wounds of those battered by life's harsh realities.

Amidst the storm's fury, Hannah felt a deep, unshakeable peace, anchored in the knowledge that she, too, was safeguarded by a covenant as enduring as the river itself. Despite its ferocity, the river would eventually return to peacefulness, mirroring the resilience and perseverance of those who found solace in their faith and heritage. Amen and Ashe.

11

2022 **Thomas Jefferson Price**

In a rather unexpected twist, Hannah received a call from her brother TJ after a long silence. He had fallen out of touch since joining the Air Force, a decision he made hastily after leaving university. His call brought news of his recent discharge from the service and his desire to start life afresh in his old hometown. That morning, TJ reached out to share that he had been discharged from the military and needed a temporary place to stay.

TJ, or Thomas Jefferson Price, was Hannah's youngest sibling, trailing her by four years. They were initially three siblings in total; however, their middle brother had tragically passed away too soon. The three young siblings had shared countless adventures under the watchful eyes of their maiden aunt, who cared for them while their parents worked long hours to provide for the family. Considering that TJ was her only remaining sibling and needed support, Hannah discussed his situation with Phillip before they agreed to open their home to TJ, hoping to offer the stability he needed to recover and start anew. Naturally, their response was affirmative.

A few days later, TJ arrived on their doorstep, visibly worn but still carrying a hint of his former spirit. His eyes, once bright, now seemed tinged with uncertainty, yet a spark of his old self, with dreams and ambitions, lingered. Hannah greeted him warmly, providing a comfortable room and a willing ear for his stories.

"Hey, Hannah! Hey, Phillip!" His rich and deep voice filled their home, breaking the silence. "It's been too long. Great to see you both!" Standing beside him, Hannah had to look up slightly; he had grown taller and broader since their last meeting. His leg injury, however, had left him with a noticeable limp, adding a hint of awkwardness to his movements.

After settling him into the guest room they had prepared, he joined them in the living room, comfortably settling into the couch, ready to describe the tumultuous journey that led him back to them. Curious and concerned, Hannah urged him to share more about his experiences.

"The Air Force's strict regimen just didn't align with my sense of independence," he explained.

His nonconformity and love for playing acid rock on his guitar often put him at odds with others, leading to disciplinary actions. Despite these conflicts, he acquired some valuable skills, like graphic design.

"A disagreement in a bar got ugly one night. I broke a man's jaw, and the police arrested me," TJ recounted. "After my release, my commanding officer recommended a general discharge without any commendation for my service."

In the wake of his discharge, TJ found himself driving home, only to fall asleep at the wheel and crash his car over a bridge, leading to an extended hospital stay due to a head injury. This accident, coupled with his limited options, led him to seek refuge with them.

"Are you alright now?" Hannah asked, concerned for his well-being.

"I get disoriented at times, but I'm getting better. I need a place to stay temporarily while I figure out my next steps. I've got nowhere else to go," he confessed.

Reflecting on TJ's past, he was once marked by good looks, intelligence, and vigor. A star on the Lewis Town High School football team and a self-taught guitarist, his life took a turn after a severe leg injury. His college years, made possible by a scholarship, were marred by loud music, frequent confrontations, and substance misuse, leading to his departure and subsequent enlistment in the Air Force. His accident brought him full circle.

In the weeks that followed, TJ gradually opened up about his ordeals—the physical pain from his injuries, the emotional distress of his discharge, and the uncertainty of his future. Hannah listened, offering encouragement and support, and together, they began to devise a plan for his recovery and reintegration.

As time passed, Hannah witnessed the re-emergence of the TJ she knew. His passion for music returned as he played his guitar, and his confidence grew with each day spent walking in the park. Their conversations shifted from past errors to future ambitions, and hope began to sparkle in his eyes once again. Reconnecting with TJ was more than just offering him shelter; it was about rekindling their sibling bond. As TJ continued on his path of healing and discovery, Hannah remained by his side, a steadfast supporter.

###

Hannah asked TJ about his plans during his recovery period, expressing genuine concern. TJ tentatively offered to contribute towards the rent if necessary. Hannah reassured him, "There's no need for that. You're our guest for now." TJ resolved to start job hunting and explore some opportunities.

Hannah suggested, hoping to ease his burden, "If you'd like, I can assist in the job search. I have several contacts that could prove beneficial. For now, though, your focus should be on recovery, enjoying nourishing meals, and getting ample rest."

As TJ settled in, the reality of his recovery period deviated from initial expectations. His days began significantly later than the rest of the household, often starting well past 10 a.m., in sharp contrast to Phillip, who started his day at 7 a.m., and Hannah, who woke at 8 a.m. to prepare breakfast on the days she didn't have to work at the hospital. TJ, known for his robust appetite, preferred a hearty breakfast of eggs, bacon, butter-rich grits, wheat toast, and milk. Initially, Hannah served him two eggs and four slices of bacon. Aware of his ongoing hunger, she increased the portions to six slices of bacon, four eggs, a sizeable serving of grits, two slices of toast, and several glasses of milk. Before eating, TJ would season his food generously with salt and pepper, and although he preferred tea over coffee, he frequently snacked on chips and soda throughout the day.

As dinner approached, it became clear that Hannah's initial estimates for adequate portions were insufficient. On one occasion, after Hannah had roasted two chickens and served them with parsley, mashed potatoes with gravy, and green beans, TJ helped himself to a substantial portion of potatoes and nearly an entire chicken while opting for a modest serving of green beans.

TJ's preference for lengthy, steam-filled showers, his liberal use of body wash, his desire for the house to be kept warm in winter and cool in summer, and his habit of watching television notably increased the household's electricity consumption. Over time, Hannah's patience began to wane. TJ's penchant for playing his guitar loudly on the days she retreated to her screened-in porch was the most upsetting intrusion. His style of music disturbed her peace.

Confronting the situation, Hannah suggested to TJ, "I believe it might be time for you to contribute towards the grocery bill. Our expenses have effectively doubled since your arrival."

TJ casually offered a twenty-dollar bill, underestimating the costs. It was clear that finding employment was essential for TJ to continue his stay.

Hannah's attempts to engage TJ with job advertisements were met with indifference, as the newspaper consistently ended up neglected beside his bed. The family dog, Sheba, a Labrador retriever, showed affection towards TJ, who unfortunately did not reciprocate. TJ even showed aggression towards the dog once, straining their relationship. Another concern was TJ's drinking habit, which continued throughout the day until he fell asleep. Hannah's concerns were disregarded despite her earnest pleas for him to seek help.

With a heavy heart, Hannah communicated a difficult decision. "TJ, it's been three months. We have not seen the progress in your recovery plan we hoped for. This situation cannot persist. I've discussed this with Aunt Grace, who has agreed to have you stay with her. You'll need to move there by Friday."

TJ responded with acceptance and gratitude. "Don't feel bad, Sis. I'm thankful for everything. I'll talk to Aunt Grace. Love you."

Thus, TJ departed from Hannah's home, marking a challenging yet necessary decision for their family and his benefit. Hannah hoped that Aunt Grace could provide the support needed for TJ to regain his footing and chart a new path forward. Despite his absence, Hannah held onto the belief in the possibility of his eventual recovery, ready to fully embrace life again.

###

Hannah discovered TJ had found a sense of belonging in the warm embrace of Aunt Grace's home, a sanctuary offered by a woman whose generosity knew no bounds. Childless by circumstance, Aunt Grace had welcomed TJ with open arms, channeling into him the depth of love and care she had reserved for the child she never had. Their evenings had been filled with the soul-stirring sounds of TJ's guitar, expressing his profound connection to the blues, creating moments of pure joy and shared contentment. Yet, despite Aunt Grace's nurturing environment, TJ's tendencies—sleeping in, enjoying hearty meals, and leisurely days punctuated by casual drinking—had remained intact. As night fell, he had often been drawn to the city's vibrant life, where fate had led him to cross paths with Candace, a woman whose life was carefree with celebration.

Compelled by Candace's festive spirit, TJ had decided to move in with her, a choice that soon revealed itself to be fraught with challenges. Petty arguments had become the norm, ranging from disputes over the last drop of milk to who adjusted the thermostat, casting a shadow over their relationship. Yet, TJ's dedication to his music, particularly his admiration for Jimmy Hendrix's electrifying guitar style, had ignited their most intense confrontations. In a moment of spite, Candace had concealed TJ's cherished guitar, an act that had escalated into a heated altercation and, regrettably, an instance of violence. The incident had prompted Candace to confide in her brother, who, outraged, had promised to get back at TJ and seek justice for his sister.

This had marked the beginning of her brother's relentless vendetta against TJ. Candace's brother had loomed as a constant threat, undermining TJ's sense of security through intimidation and destructive acts. Yielding to her brother's insistence, Candace had taken legal measures, obtaining a restraining order that barred TJ from their residence. Confronted with unending strife, TJ had decided to seek solace and opportunity elsewhere, setting his sights on the distant promise of Los Angeles—a city synonymous with the allure of musical success.

With a heavy heart yet driven by the hope of reinvention and the allure of new beginnings, TJ had embarked on his journey to Los Angeles. He had left behind a stormy chapter of his life, stepping into the unknown with a resolve to rewrite his story, inspired by the dream of achieving musical recognition and pursuing a future yet to be shaped.

###

Upon his arrival in Los Angeles, TJ was homeless and struggling not only with survival but also with racial disparities that complicated his daily existence. He was more vulnerable to discrimination and violence and had limited access to crucial resources. The fear of being unfairly targeted by the police because of his race was a constant worry for him, heightening his sense of vulnerability. Health care and mental support were also complex to come by, adding to the hurdles he had to overcome.

TJ depended on homeless shelters and soup kitchens for his hygiene and meals. His situation made him a target for exploitation by those who took advantage of the vulnerable. To safeguard his prized guitar, he kept it locked in a bus station locker, but his other belongings were unprotected and often stolen.

TJ's life took harsher turns when he was robbed and assaulted twice, which left him with severe injuries, including a perforated eardrum, a detached cornea, and a fractured tibia. These injuries resulted in permanent disabilities: he lost hearing in one ear, sight in one eye, and walked with a pronounced limp. After enduring two months of relentless hardship in Los Angeles, the accumulation of physical injuries, emotional trauma, and systemic barriers nearly pushed TJ to the brink of despair. His life was a stark illustration of the intricate connections between homelessness, racial injustice, and the quest for dignity and safety.

One day, Pastor Jeff Grady led a group of missionaries to the shelter where TJ was staying. They brought clothes and food, and Pastor Grady felt a solid connection to TJ. He invited him to join their Sunday worship. TJ was hesitant at first and worried about not having the right clothes. Understanding his concerns, Pastor Grady ensured TJ received a suit and shoes the following day and arranged a shuttle bus to take him to the church for the service.

Progressive Church stood as a prime example of what is affectionately known as the "Black Church," a term theologian Delores Williams coined to capture the essence of an institution deeply rooted in the history and spirit of Black communities. These establishments are far more than mere venues for worship; they act as strongholds of endurance against systemic injustices. They provide both spiritual counsel and tangible assistance to those in dire straits. For someone like TJ, struggling to find his footing, the church offered a glimmer of hope and a place of spiritual refuge.

Following the morning worship, the church elders arranged a communal meal, further welcoming TJ in a warm embrace of inclusion and safety. This heartfelt welcome and the sense of community he found at Progressive Church deeply moved TJ, compelling him to join the congregation. In a meaningful display of commitment, TJ retrieved his guitar from a locker at the bus station, signaling his eagerness to contribute his musical abilities to the church's services. From then on, TJ was a regular presence at Progressive Church, sharing his gift of music and dedicating his talents to glorifying the Lord.

###

Hannah and TJ had started to reconnect more frequently, deliberately attempting to close the distance that had expanded during the years they had drifted apart. Their conversations naturally veered toward childhood reminiscences and a longing for the past. One week, nostalgia took them even further back.

"Do you remember that day we decided to play Tarzan in the peach tree out back?" Hannah began, recalling a cherished memory. Like skeleton bones, the tree's sprawling limbs guaranteed no peaches would fall. Their brother, who was sturdy and elegant, climbed up first. The sunlight bathed his face, giving his skin a rich, chocolate glow. He grasped the rope that perpetually hung there and bellowed like Tarzan as he swung to the ground, eliciting screams of delight from everyone.

"Next, it was my turn," Hannah chimed in. That day, she had glanced toward the kitchen to ensure their mother wasn't watching, as she had often warned Hannah about climbing trees and scarring her knees.

"It's just not proper for a young girl to climb trees," their mother scolded.

Despite propriety, Hannah's adrenaline surged as she swung down swiftly, mimicking her brother's yell and perfect arch.

"Then, it was your turn, TJ. You were the youngest, and climbing the tree took a long time. At last, you grabbed the rope and began your Tarzan screech," Hannah recounted. "Just then, everyone heard a crack and looked up in time to see the limb crashing to the ground with you still attached."

"Yep. That's when Mom looked out the window and yelled for us to get out of that tree!"

###

One Saturday afternoon, after Hannah had completed all her chores, she called TJ to see if he was interested in a conversation. TJ shared with her that he had been reflecting on their father recently.

"Daddy was a violent man, for sure," TJ remarked. "I think one of the reasons I am so messed up is because Daddy was not a good role model. As a young boy, I looked to him to show me what a man was supposed to do. I think I got my tendency to drink too much by watching Daddy."

"You're right. Daddy was always involved in some drama or other," Hannah recounted the incidents as she remembered them.

Strange events often occurred with their father on the weekends. One particular Saturday, as they were playing outside, a wire fence that separated their yard from the neighbor's caught their attention. Pale pink and white morning glories wove through the honeycomb pattern of the wire. The three siblings, at eight, seven, and five years old, came tearing around the corner, chasing each other with sticks and making a lot of noise. As they neared the grassy strip between the fence and the house, they noticed a body slumped over the fence, causing it to cave in slightly. Curious, they tiptoed toward the lifeless figure, wondering if he was alive or had been shot. It did not take long for them to realize that the body was that of their father. He had stumbled home the night before from Alexander's Tavern up the street and had made it only as far as the fence that marked their property line.

"We ran inside to tell our mother," TJ said. "Without a word, she and Granddaddy dragged him inside the house. No one spoke of the incident after that day."

"To make matters scary," Hannah added, "Daddy exploited his morbid fascination with guns. He was a hunter and often went on multi-day trips, returning with his packs laden with squirrel, rabbit, or pheasant. One time, he even brought home some venison. He probably didn't kill the deer himself. Who knows how he came into possession of the meat? No one was bold enough to ask out loud. He was the one with the gun. He was the man."

TJ said, "Daddy had a German pistol, which he obtained as a veteran of the Korean War. I was never sure what his job had been in the military, but whatever it was, it created in him a fascination with guns."

"He used to stand on the front lawn of our home and shoot at the moon until the gun was empty," Hannah recalled. "When the police arrived, he disavowed any knowledge of having heard shots or having seen anything strange taking place in the neighborhood."

"On other occasions, especially when he was drunk, he simply shot at the stars for the sport of it. During these episodes, our mother disappeared to her room and closed the door she locked behind her," TJ said.

Hannah didn't say this to TJ, but after witnessing how their father treated their mother, she watched over their mother and tried to be as close as possible. She wanted to protect her, but there was no way she could.

###

Hannah and TJ often spent hours discussing their father's painful history. TJ recounted their father's job at the leather tanning plant. Their father had been a dedicated employee, commuting to his job at the Northrup Leather Tanning Company in Harbor Point, a charming town on the shores of Lake Michigan. With a recent manufacturing boom, its population increased by 75 percent, drawing Blacks and Southern Whites seeking better prospects. The tannery, a key component of Harbor Point's industrial framework, had actively recruited Southern Blacks during World War II and had even built housing for them amidst widespread racial discrimination. Their father started working at the plant in 1955.

Though he started as a general laborer, their father harbored ambitions of rising to a managerial position. Blessed with a creative mind, he consistently sought ways to enhance efficiency and innovate. The company required promotional exams, which he passed with flying colors, yet he was consistently overlooked for advancement due to ever-changing criteria. Nevertheless, his enthusiasm for the leather-tanning craft persisted. He was fascinated by transforming raw hides into leather despite the environmental risks and the complex use of chemicals like chromium sulfate. Unfazed by his lack of career advancement, he concentrated on developing a waste management technique that used microbes to reduce metal concentrations in wastewater.

When the company's management rejected his proposal to improve environmental practices, not for its lack of merit but because of racial prejudice, he was heartbroken yet resolute. He scrutinized the company's practices and observed them illegally discharging chromium-laden wastewater into Lake Michigan. His efforts to document the illegal dumping were foiled when the perpetrators spotted him.

The situation quickly escalated, leading to a mysterious fire at the tannery. The managers suspected that Daddy had sabotaged the plant. Although their father proclaimed his innocence, a violent confrontation ensued. The skirmish concluded with gunfire, and their father wounded one of the assailants, which ultimately led to their father's arrest and harsh treatment by the police. These events profoundly scarred him.

###

As she sat quietly, the memories of her father enveloped her like a soft, yet persistent, mist. He had been a man of profound intellect and grand aspirations, but life seemed to conspire against him, tethering his spirit with chains of racism and entrenched poverty. Each day, he bore these injustices like open wounds, and she watched helplessly as his wounds consumed him from within. The weight of the world eventually proved too heavy, and when she was just ten, her father chose to end his battle with a world that wouldn't let him rise. His suicide left a void filled with echoing anger and unresolved grief.

Her father had been a rebel, his heart ablaze with a fierce desire to challenge the status quo. She remembered the nights he would step out into the darkness, his silhouette framed against the moonlight, shooting at the moon and stars in symbolic defiance. This raw display of frustration and despair had frightened her as a child. Yet, in those moments of rebellion, she believed she learned something vital about resisting the cages society tried to place around them.

Despite the turmoil, her love for her father had never waned. It endured, tinged with sadness and a complex tapestry of remorse. His spirit lingered, a constant reminder of where she came from and the battles they both inherited. The societal expectations were clear and grim: they did not expect his children to thrive. She had dedicated her life to proving them wrong, to honor the dreams her father could not fulfill.

She vaguely recalled scripture suggesting the sins of the father are visited upon the children of the third and fourth generations. These words often led her to wonder—had she suffered sufficiently from the legacies of pain and struggle passed down through her bloodline? Yet, in her quieter moments of reflection, she realized that her father's life, his struggles, and his end shaped not just a narrative of sorrow but one of enduring love and resilience. This realization steadied her heart, urging her to transform the scars into stars, to turn the pain into purpose. As she continued this journey, she carried her father's spirit, dreams, and battles as both a beacon and a warning. Hannah prayed that his spirit would rest in peace. Amen and Ashe.

12

2022 The Woman of His Dreams

Throughout numerous phone conversations, TJ consistently updated Hannah on his life in Los Angeles. His gospel ensemble soared in popularity, leading to performances in various regional churches. Transitioning from a style reminiscent of acid rock to the heart and soul of classic gospel and Christian hymns, TJ's voice, known for its rich depth and clarity, infused life into beloved songs, captivating audiences everywhere.

About a year after TJ had joined the church, he met Keisha, a bubbly woman who visited the Progressive Church with a friend. With a voice potent enough to stir souls, her visiting performance with the praise team was nothing short of electrifying, mesmerizing the audience with her innate talent and emotional depth. Offstage, Keisha's warmth and genuine nature, complemented by her infectious laughter, endeared her to everyone. She became a steadfast supporter of TJ and his aspirations. Their collaborative efforts in music not only brought them closer on a personal level but also elevated their professional partnership. Keisha's admiration and respect for TJ were evident, a testament to her love and belief in his talent and dedication.

Facing the music industry's ups and downs, Keisha and TJ celebrated their victories and learned from their challenges. Their unwavering love for each other was a cornerstone of strength and inspiration as they pursued their dreams. Keisha's influence in TJ's life was a constant reminder of the transformative power of love and music. Their music together, bolstered by strategic promotion, started gaining traction on local radio stations, prompting them to consider an album. Their professional success matched the deepening of their romantic relationship, a love that TJ found unparalleled. They settled into a cozy home, embracing a life of love, music, and, admittedly, a penchant for indulgent cuisine.

Pastor Grady, ever supportive, introduced TJ to Juan Carlos, a local graphic artist. Juan Carlos offered TJ office space, aiding his graphic design business and growing musical reputation. TJ also became a central figure in the church, assuming roles as a deacon and music ministry director. His musical ventures with Keisha, especially in blues, were promising.

Hannah and Phillip eagerly anticipated Keisha and TJ's visit during Thanksgiving. Keisha's culinary talents were a highlight, and her dishes were a delicious blend of her passion for cooking and holiday traditions. One evening, Keisha shared her past struggles, including her painful decision to leave her daughter for music, leading to family estrangement, and her battle with breast cancer. During her story, Keisha revealed her hesitance to marry TJ due to her health concerns.

###

Despite the clock nearing midnight, Hannah woke up, never knowing who was on the other end at that hour of the night.

"Hey, Hannah, this is TJ. How are you doing?" TJ's voice came through the phone.

It hadn't occurred to him there was a three-hour time difference between their cities.

"I'm doing well, thanks. What's up?" Hannah replied, her voice steady despite the late hour.

"I'm in the hospital. Suffered a heart attack, unfortunately." TJ's tone was somber.

"Oh, my! How long have you been there?" Concern laced Hannah's words.

"I've been here for two weeks. The medical team inserted two stents into my arteries."

TJ further explained that the doctors suggested a lifestyle overhaul was crucial for his survival. He needed to cut out alcohol, overhaul his diet, and quit smoking. He also needed to adjust his late-night schedule.

"They've started me on new heart medication. I'm also on antidepressants and medications for anxiety. I believe my ongoing frustrations with the VA triggered the heart attack." TJ continued, revealing that he had been in touch with a legal advisor to help claim disability payments stemming from the accident when his car went off the bridge.

"My lawyer believes that with sufficient evidence, the military might have to compensate me with back pay. The problem is that the military is denying that my crash was the cause of my ongoing medical problems, and they are refusing to compensate me for my injuries." TJ's frustration was palpable.

"Your prayers would mean a lot to me. You're the best prayer warrior I know."

"Of course." Right then and there, Hannah offered prayers over the phone.

"Thanks, Sis. I feel I can finally rest now." Their communication became more regular after that. TJ updated her on his legal battle with the military, his efforts to launch a new graphic design venture, and his music composition for an upcoming album.

###

Keisha was out of town attending to family business, so Phillip and Hannah decided to visit TJ in Los Angeles. Upon arrival, they were greeted by a visibly tired yet welcoming TJ. Despite his exhaustion, he graciously assumed the role of their host and tour guide, ensuring they experienced the best of the city.

Their exploration included a drive along the iconic Crenshaw Boulevard, a street framed by majestic palm trees and historic towers, showcasing the neighborhood's rich African American heritage. Notably, Crenshaw is dotted with parks and green spaces, fostering community and offering residents and visitors spaces for outdoor enjoyment and social gatherings. They ended their day of urban exploration at a relaxed backyard barbecue at TJ's residence.

As the evening drew to a close, they found themselves enveloped in the lingering warmth of the setting sun. TJ's backyard, a private oasis with a concrete patio brought to life by flower beds lining the fence, felt comfortable and safe. A thoughtful touch included a small gate in the fence for the neighborhood cats, a testament to Keisha and TJ's kindness towards animals. Their charming and relatively well-fed cat, Fluffy, joined the party, adding to the cozy atmosphere as they sipped on soft drinks and engaged in easy conversation.

###

In one of their subsequent telephone conversations, TJ informed Hannah that Keisha was facing renewed health challenges.

"Between the two of us, we spend much time at doctor's appointments. Since we don't have a car, we rely on public transportation," he said.

TJ explained that folks from Progressive Church occasionally offered rides, especially Pastor Grady, who helped them whenever needed. The church deacons also looked out for them, sending over healthy treats every week and caring for their lawn.

"Is there any way I can help?" Hannah asked, knowing she could do little for them being so far away.

"No, I think we're okay at this end. Please, keep us in your prayers."

"I most certainly will." After ending the call, Hannah prayed fervently, asking for continuous blessings and grace upon them. Out of concern for them in LA, she started sending them greeting cards, humorous texts, and thoughtful gifts to lift their spirits.

###

Six months after their prior conversation, TJ's midnight call startled Hannah.

"Hey, Hannah, it's TJ. How are you doing?"

"I'm good. What's going on?"

"Keisha's cancer is back. She went in for a checkup, and the x-ray showed that cancer had metastasized. It's now affecting her lungs and kidneys. I'll keep you posted."

A couple of days later, TJ called back.

"Hey, Hannah, it's TJ. Keisha died. Her kidneys stopped working. She was so bloated you could hardly recognize her." TJ's voice sounded stressed.

"I am so sorry to hear that. How can I support you?"

"Can you write her obituary?"

"Yes. I will send it to you by Friday. Please send me some pictures and a few details about her life. I am happy to help."

###

Keisha Young, the youngest of six children, was born in Kansas City, Missouri, where she attended public schools. During her formative years, she cultivated her faith and, over time, developed an unshakable love of God and an unwavering devotion to Jesus Christ.

Keisha moved to Los Angeles, California, to follow her dreams. She completed her formal education at Providence College, where she prepared herself to work in the healthcare profession. After earning her degree, she served as a respiratory therapist for over thirty years. She frequently expressed concern for both the physical needs and spiritual well-being of the people who were under her care. Several people have remarked on how deeply she touched their lives.

While in LA, Keisha entered a relationship with Thomas Jefferson Price, also known as TJ. They shared a life of devotion for more than eighteen years. In both her actions and her words, Keisha conveyed that the two of them completed each other. Over time, they became one another's light in a world sometimes dimmed by darkness. Keisha and TJ were caregivers, friends, companions, and prayer partners to each other. Their mutual love and loyalty were nothing short of remarkable.

Keisha was a gifted musician and enjoyed touching people's lives through her vocational calling as a singer, songwriter, and music composer. She was a member of ASCAP and was constantly involved in musical projects. Although her skills spanned several musical genres, her ongoing aspiration was to produce a gospel music compilation.

Sewing represented another one of Keisha's passions. At any given time, she could be found pressing one of her three sewing machines into service to produce formal gowns, casual dresses, pantsuits, and other attire. When she wasn't writing music or sewing, she enjoyed caring for her cat, Fluffy.

Keisha made her transition to her heavenly home after an extended illness. She leaves to cherish her memory her beloved companion TJ, her sister-in-law, and a host of friends. Keisha's parents and her daughter preceded her in death. She will be interred at Englewood Cemetery. Keisha will live on in our hearts and our minds.

###

In the ensuing months, TJ and Hannah spent many hours in conversation. Their bond deepened as TJ sought ways to fill the void left by Keisha. Loneliness drove him to immerse himself more in his graphic design work. Despite his efforts to maintain sobriety, the grief led him back to alcohol for comfort. His eating habits deteriorated, favoring foods high in cholesterol and saturated fats, resulting in a weight gain of twenty pounds.

TJ also ventured into the digital world, occasionally falling prey to internet scams. Once, he excitedly shared with Hannah an email claiming he had won ten million dollars from a company in Nigeria, requiring only his personal information to claim the prize. Hannah advised him to recognize the deceit. Another scam involved a fraudulent check for supposed services, which led to his account being debited when the check bounced. A fictitious credit card company also tried to extract his personal information under the pretext of preventing fraud. Fortunately, TJ soon learned to discern these fraudulent schemes as exploitative attempts.

###

TJ had dedicated countless hours to refining his guitar skills, recording his performances, and sharing them with potential agents. He was diligent in his songwriting and sought to perfect his music for a prospective album, engaging with agents who promised to propel his career forward. His musical journey had taken him to various churches alongside his pastor, gradually building his reputation as a talented musician. His pursuits had also led him to nightclubs, where he soon regressed deeper into his old habits.

During this time, TJ formed a friendship with one of the Elders at Progressive Church, who decided to look after him. The elder's granddaughter, Delilah, who had a child from a previous relationship, had recently been in a financially dependent relationship that ended with the older companion's death. Now, she was seeking new companionship. Her loneliness had motivated her to begin attending the church with her grandmother again. TJ met Delilah at a church dinner and soon started dating her, their relationship quickly escalating from dinners and movies to more intimate encounters.

When TJ told Hannah about Delilah, she suspected Delilah's motives were less than honorable. From TJ's descriptions of the relationship, Hannah surmised that while TJ sought companionship, Delilah sought someone to care for her material needs. Her demand for gifts had gradually increased from small tokens of affection to more extravagant requests, leading TJ to try to fulfill even her most lavish desires.

"Man, you better put on your gym shoes and run the other way!" Hannah warned her brother.

Despite Hannah's warnings, TJ and Delilah married. The couple had appeared genuinely content for a while, as evidenced by their joyful photographs online.

However, the relationship took a different turn when TJ received a substantial settlement from the military for a previously unacknowledged injury, ensuring financial security for life. Delilah's true colors became more apparent as she grew more controlling and manipulative, using TJ's vulnerability and health issues to her advantage. She seemed more interested in his financial resources than his well-being, and their marriage became more strained as TJ realized her selfishness.

Delilah quickly devised plans for TJ's newfound wealth, prioritizing her education, her son's private schooling, and the purchase of a suburban home far from TJ's usual haunts. TJ acquiesced to Delilah's wishes to make her happy. His life soon became a balancing act between his commitments and his deteriorating health, exacerbated by loneliness and a return to unhealthy habits.

Delilah and her son moved into their new suburban home. Because TJ's medical support system and graphic design job were in the city, he did not move in with them immediately. Delilah promised they would be together again after her son graduated from high school in two years. Until then, she would check on TJ on her way from work. Delilah's visits had become sporadic, with her stopping in to check on him twice a week before taking off to pursue her self-improvement at TJ's expense.

It was time for TJ's annual checkup. He took public transportation to his appointment at the medical center. When he arrived, the doctors admitted him immediately. He had suffered a heart attack and needed bypass surgery. His heart stopped once while he was under anesthesia, but the doctors managed to bring him back. Delilah didn't arrive at the hospital to check on her husband until the next day. TJ's hospital stay was lengthy as he went through cardiac rehabilitation. After months of care, the hospital released TJ to go home. Delilah continued her sporadic visit schedule, even though her husband seriously needed her presence and care. During his conversations with Hannah, TJ shared that he had repeatedly asked Delilah for a divorce, but she refused to grant the request.

Delilah invited her extended family to her suburban home for a holiday feast the following Thanksgiving. She informed TJ she didn't have time to pick him up, so she would arrange for her aunt to drop a plate at his house after the celebration. Delilah had dropped in to check on TJ early the next week and found him lying dead on the sofa.

###

When Delilah informed Hannah of TJ's death, Hannah was overwhelmed by a mix of sorrow and anger. Delilah's exploitation and neglect had contributed to the tragic end of a life that had once been filled with promise. Due to COVID-19 travel restrictions, Hannah was unable to attend TJ's funeral in person, leaving her to mourn from afar and reflect on the profound impact of Delilah's selfishness and TJ's loss. Sitting in the quiet darkness, Hannah had no more tears to cry.

The depth of Hannah's sadness was ineffable. She sat at her desk while her emotions rested heavily on her shoulders. She decided the only way she could handle the loss of her brother was to write him a letter. As she sat there, she reflected on their lives. In the last few years, TJ and Hannah grew closer together through their frequent conversations and the reconstruction of their past lives. TJ and Hannah had benefited from a closer look at what shaped them. It had occurred to Hannah that she and TJ had often deceived themselves into believing they were looking at one thing, but on closer inspection, they realized they were mistaken. They thought they were seeing something noble and lofty, but they started to see its stress, cracks, and fissures upon closer inspection. They initially thought they had lived a fairytale life as children, yet on closer inspection, the optical illusion shifted, revealing a life of poverty and desperation.

###

Hannah sat immersed in contemplation as she waited for something unknown to assuage the tender wounds of her grief. Her brother TJ had left this earthly realm, leaving a void too profound to articulate. In these quiet moments, a soft yet persistent inner voice led Hannah through the maze of her memories and grief.

Reflecting on their childhood, Hannah realized how adverse experiences shaped her adult existence. It became apparent that her constant quest for new understandings, insatiable curiosity, and inherent empathy were not just aspects of her identity. These traits evolved into the tools of a wounded healer, transforming personal anguish into a source of strength for others. In her efforts to uplift those around her, Hannah realized that her life blossomed in unforeseen ways. Her ministry, a mirror of her most profound beliefs, fortified her, granting her the resilience to support the vast weight of compassion that had accompanied her since she first felt the call to serve.

It was through sharing TJ's struggles that she gained a clearer perspective. His journey, marked by suffering and overshadowed by sadness, revealed a profound truth and a light formidable enough to illuminate her way forward. With a grateful and heavy heart, she told TJ, "I'm sorry for the profound pain you endured, my dear brother. Forgive me for not being there to lighten your load." In honoring TJ's memory, Hannah pledged to be a pillar of comfort and strength, just as her ancestors had been for her. Through this reflection, she moved forward, mindful of the past, yet with her gaze set on the hope of healing other hearts as she continued to heal her own. Amen and Ashe.

13

2022 Hannah's Ancestors

If Hannah's ancestors taught her nothing else, they taught her to endure, to fill her life with distractions, to minimize hurt, and to maximize her will to survive. Hannah often hid behind the shelving unit that divided the living room from the dining room and watched her mother folding laundry pulled from the linen bags, still warm from the processing plant. Sending out the family's laundry was the only luxury her mother afforded herself. Hannah hated doing laundry because her mother had spoiled her, and she loved her for it, permitting Hannah to hold onto this small concession for herself. As a little girl, Hannah was afraid for her mother. From her hiding place, she sometimes saw her father hit her mother. She saw her mother cry but was too afraid to come out and hug her, to tell her that things would be alright. Hannah wanted her mother to be happy and safe. She was deeply sorry that her father did those things to her mother.

Her mother's capacity for survival was a remarkable feat, considering that she navigated a world fraught with racial and gender-based challenges. Moreover, she was both a victim and a survivor of domestic abuse. Like her contemporaries, her mother honed her ability to endure by cultivating a resilient spirit and an unyielding inner strength. Embracing endurance often meant presenting a facade of strength and pushing onward, regardless of the hurdles. However, the necessity of endurance often fostered a sense of solitude, as she felt compelled to shoulder her burdens in isolation.

Hannah's faith also was a legacy from her mother. Despite the adversities and challenges she faced as a Black woman, her mother's faith in God never wavered. She encountered many hardships that could have led her to despair, yet she clung to her hope with unwavering conviction. She was adamant about integrating faith into their upbringing, ensuring her children were at church whenever the doors were open, with Bibles in hand. Hannah still cherished the black, leather-bound Bible she received from the evangelist when she was seven and baptized. They had to memorize verses from the King James Bible and recite them in front of everyone after Sunday school.

During Sunday morning sermons, the preacher fervently declared that they were all sinners in the hands of an angry God. It seemed like everything was a sin back then. At the same time, Hannah recalled the preacher's dedication to making the scripture accessible, especially for those in the congregation who couldn't read. The sermons followed a careful structure—scripture reading, elucidation, and application boiled down to three memorable points and a celebration of God's blessings. The sermons often reminded them that just as God delivered the chosen people from bondage, God would deliver them because they were chosen, too.

The music mostly revolved around their struggles, perseverance, grace, mercy, faithfulness, and healing themes. The hymns on Sunday mornings were powerful. The services were filled with lively expressions of faith—shouting, clapping, and dancing. Many songs resonated with them sincerely, portraying Jesus as their Redeemer who understood their sorrows and pains because He had faced similar afflictions.

###

Hannah sat at her kitchen table, her eyes lighting up with warmth and wisdom as she shared her thoughts with her friend Indigo.

"You know, Indigo, when I think about how Black women have interacted with the Bible throughout history, it's truly profound. Our ancestors didn't just read the scriptures passively; they embraced them with faith and trust that transformed their lives."

Hannah's voice was soft yet emphatic as she continued.

"Imagine the strength it took for these women, including our mothers, to see themselves as part of God's covenant, especially when the world offered them little protection or reason for hope. They redefined their reality through this lens of love and grace, believing fiercely that God's promises were also meant for them."

Indigo nodded, absorbing every word as Hannah continued, "This belief wasn't just comforting; it was empowering. Black women envisioned a God who was the Lord of Hosts, a commander of an endless celestial army, ready to defend them at all costs. This is the God who led the Israelites out of Egypt with powerful miracles and who sustained them through their exile in Babylon. Just as God healed and protected the oppressed and wounded in those ancient times, they trusted God to do the same for them."

Hannah's eyes shone passionately as she spoke of these women's deep, personal connection with God.

"Our mothers and grandmothers found a God big enough to face any adversity, strong enough to bring them through hostile environments. Understanding God as a protector and healer gave them the strength to endure and the courage to hope."

She smiled at Indigo with her heart full. "It's a legacy of faith that teaches us, even today, that no matter the struggle, we are never alone. If God could love and protect our ancestors, She surely could love and protect us, too, healing our wounds and guiding us through our challenges."

Indigo reached out, squeezing Hannah's hand in a silent thank you for sharing such powerful reflections.

###

Hannah had come to perceive her existence through the lens of her foremothers, who had endured the horrors of slavery and other unspeakable acts of violence. The wisdom she drew upon was forged from a cauldron filled with pain, anger, and despair, a wisdom that was also deeply rooted in the scriptures that guided her. Living at the complex junction of confounding social variables, Hannah had developed a profound understanding of suffering. This insight was not merely intellectual but woven through the fabric of her being, learned through the conditioning passed down from generations of resilient women before her.

Hannah felt deeply connected to the collective consciousness of her ancestors, finding God in all things and often in the most unexpected places. This shared consciousness, a blend of knowledge and survival tactics specific to her community, had endowed her with resilience. It was a resilience from a shared epistemology and a theological hope handed down by female ancestors who had stood where she stood now. Hannah had sought God with her whole being and found God's presence in life's simple, everyday miracles—the cry of a newborn, the sunset's glow, the rush of river currents. Hannah firmly believed that God manifested in her life in various forms, meeting her at her point of need with solace and healing. Above all, she was buoyed by the unshakable knowledge of God's limitless, unconditional love, which empowered her to love herself wholly.

In her self-awareness, Hannah saw the image of God reflected in the faces of those she served. She recognized God in the weary eyes of the oppressed, sharing their sorrows and joys. To Hannah, every face reflected the Divine, and she did not limit the possibilities of God's presence. Recently, she had embraced the idea that her brokenness was a tool God used to minister to others.

Hannah's life was a testament to the power of faith amid relentless adversity. Her pathway to healing was communal, supported by strong women, counselors, spiritual leaders, and a network that embraced her wholly. Her deep emotional reserves, born from personal pain, now fueled her empathy and compassion. Hannah's faith was her sanctuary, providing comfort and a profound connection to God, sustaining her in despair and elevating her joy. Her identity was markedly shaped by her intersectional reality—race, gender, and spirituality—which informed her unique experiences and challenges. Within her community, Hannah found not just solace but also empowerment. These connections were crucial, offering understanding, compassion, and celebration. Moreover, despite her wounds, Hannah remained a staunch advocate for justice, championing racial equality, gender empowerment, and social change, seeing this advocacy as an extension of her faith.

###

Hannah needed a respite. She decided to accompany Phillip on a business trip to Burlington, Vermont, during the enchanting autumn season. As Phillip immersed himself in conference meetings throughout the daylight hours, Hannah embarked on explorations that allowed her to savor Burlington's captivating attractions. Her wanderlust led her to the University of Vermont campus, where she visited its library. A detour to Ben and Jerry's capped off her afternoon with the simple pleasure of a creamy ice cream cone. Her evening wound down amidst the festivities of Octoberfest, where she indulged in the local fare of succulent wieners and sauerkraut.

Phillip and Hannah culminated their Burlington visit with a serenely beautiful sunset cruise on Lake Champlain, which is highly recommended for its autumnal spectacle. As they embarked upon this tranquil voyage, the canvas of the sky transformed into a mesmerizing palette of oranges, pinks, and purples mirrored by the lake's surface in a dazzling display of nature's artistry.

Gliding across the waters of Lake Champlain, the gentle caress of the waves lulled them into a state of profound relaxation. At the same time, the crispness of the fall air invited them to embrace each other in a cocoon of peace and tranquility. As the sun began to set, the horizon glowed with a golden radiance, enhancing the vibrancy of the lakeside foliage. This natural spectacle seemed to elevate them beyond the mundane, leaving them feeling refreshed and at peace as the cruise gently returned to shore. The day's earlier stresses gave way to a rejuvenating calm that promised to linger in their memories as a cherished highlight of their celebration.

###

From her perch on the porch, Hannah gazed at the tranquil river gracefully flowing a short distance away. The serene waters, reflecting the soft hues of the sky, brought a sense of peace that enveloped her. In this moment of quiet reflection, Hannah felt a profound connection to the Divine Spirit, whose presence, though not physical, wrapped around her with the warmth of ages and the urgency of a cry for justice.

Hannah acknowledged the omnipresence of God. A recent insight had struck her with particular force: her imperfections were not merely flaws but vessels through which God's healing could reach others in their moments of brokenness. The trials stemming from her history, culture, and unwavering faith had uniquely shaped her path as a woman of faith and a Black woman—with resilience as her constant companion. Her identity, richly woven from the threads of her race, gender, and spirituality, formed a beautiful, though often complex, tapestry. Each experience of discrimination and marginalization tested her, honed her resolve, and clarified her purpose. Amen and Ashe.

14

2023 **Advocates for Change**

Hannah, Indigo, and Roberta met for lunch one Saturday at Clara's Kitchen, known for its soul food offerings. It was one of the only business establishments that survived after the urban renewal project bulldozed over most of the south-side homes and establishments. The restaurant was comfortable, and its smells and ambiance reminded them of their grandmothers' kitchens. They selected a light fare consisting of seafood gumbo and salad, cornbread, and sweet tea.

Indigo enthusiastically started the brainstorming session: "Hey, everyone, I'd like to talk about ways we, as Black women, can truly impact our communities. What do you think?"

Hannah's eyes were bright with ideas. "It's about creating robust networks where we share resources, provide support, and collectively tackle the challenges we face."

Roberta's voice was filled with passion. "And it's not just about personal support, right? We need to concern ourselves with larger societal issues. We've got to stand up for social justice and push for racial equity."

"Absolutely," Indigo replied, her gaze intense. "Advocating for systemic change is crucial. It's all about dismantling oppression and building a fairer world for our children and their children."

Hannah smiled, her mind racing with possibilities. "Speaking of future generations, what about mentorship? Imagine the impact if each of us dedicated time to mentor young Black girls, equipping them with the necessary tools and confidence to succeed."

"That's a powerful idea," Indigo agreed, her voice hopeful. "Investing in their education and leadership skills could reshape their future. It's about opening doors that might not otherwise be available to them."

Roberta nodded enthusiastically. "And let's not forget economic empowerment. We should encourage support for Black-owned businesses. It's a direct way to boost economic vitality within our community."

"Exactly," Hannah added. "Supporting Black entrepreneurs helps individual businesses and strengthens our entire community financially. It creates a thriving economic ecosystem where everyone benefits."

Indigo leaned forward, her expression turning contemplative. "And we must remember the importance of self-care and healing. We can't effectively contribute if we're not taking care of ourselves. Our mental health and well-being are crucial."

"So true," Roberta agreed. "Self-care empowers us to sustain our efforts in supporting our families and fighting for justice."

Hannah's voice was warm and affectionate. "Fostering our intergenerational connections is invaluable. So much wisdom is in our traditions and stories, which can empower and strengthen us."

"It's like weaving a rich tapestry," Indigo reflected. "These connections between generations preserve our culture and values, providing strength and continuity for our community."

"Exactly, Hannah. It feels like there's so much we can do, both individually and collectively," Indigo concluded, her eyes alight with determination.

"Yes," Hannah responded, her tone resolute. "It's up to us to make a difference, and I truly believe we can. Now that we've identified the issues, let's go out and change the world."

###

In the small community of Lewis Town, a place marked by diverse demographics and deep-seated issues, the air was thick with tension that had built over the years. It was a community woven together by systemic struggles and individual grievances, compounded by an economy that seemed to falter more with each passing day. Feeling neglected and frustrated, the residents were a powder keg waiting for a spark.

That spark came in the form of the violent riots that erupted in the recent past, shaking the town to its very core. Days were filled with chaos: storefronts were smashed, businesses looted, and the streets that once echoed with the laughter of playing children were now scenes of turmoil. The fabric of Lewis Town, once so vibrant, seemed irrevocably frayed. As the dust settled and the reality of destruction and loss dawned in the aftermath, the town was in a collective state of mourning.

It was during these sad days that Hannah stepped forward. Known and respected in the community, she suffered losses that resonated deeply with her neighbors. When she spoke of recovery and change, her voice carried not just authority but a shared experience of grief. With a blend of resolve and compassion, Hannah proposed a bold idea.

"What if we could come together to address the symptoms of our troubles and their roots? I propose that the City Council form a Task Force to study our concerns," she said.

Thus, the Lewis Town Task Force for Change was born. Under Hannah's guidance and with the involvement of other local leaders, activists, law enforcement officials, business owners, and educators, the task force tackled the issues head-on. They aimed to facilitate dialogue across the community's spectrum, reform policing practices to build trust and safety, enhance economic opportunities to invigorate the local economy and create a more inclusive and equitable environment for all its residents.

###

The Task Force quickly became a beacon of hope. Meetings were held, plans were drawn up, and slowly but surely, the community began to examine the underlying issues. There would be no return to the status quo but a bold stride into a future where the current brand of despair and destruction would never find such fertile ground again. The newly formed Lewis Town Task Force for Change convened their first official meeting with a tangible sense of gravity about the work ahead. The city council selected Hannah, Indigo, Roberta, Paul, and Zach to explore and address the deep-seated issues underlying local conflicts.

Hannah opened the meeting by emphasizing the profound importance of their mission: to heal the deep wounds within the community and knit together a fabric of unity and peace amidst the lingering aftershocks of recent turmoil. Their goal was ambitious—not merely to rebuild but to transform Lewis Town into a beacon of resilience, justice, and harmony for the future.

"We should focus on what will help our community heal and progress." Hannah set the tone with her enthusiasm.

On a sober note, Indigo added, "Key to our success is open and honest communication. We should set up forums for dialogue where everyone can voice their concerns, share their pains, and, more crucially, listen to one another with empathy and understanding. We should foster safe spaces where healing conversations can take place."

Paul, nodding in agreement, responded, "Exactly, Indigo. Building these communicative bridges and nurturing reconciliation is vital. We have to create opportunities for dialogue and collaboration that delve into the root causes of our recent disturbances, not just the superficial symptoms."

Roberta added, "This means confronting and addressing the systemic inequalities that have fueled unrest. We're tasked with creating an inclusive environment that serves all residents of Lewis Town."

Zach, listening intently, said, "And let's remember the power of community involvement. We should encourage local organizations, leaders, and citizens to collaborate toward common goals. This collective effort is essential for building solidarity and reinforcing unity."

Hannah reflected on their input and added, "It's also crucial that we empower our residents to be part of these decision-making processes. When people feel involved, they develop a sense of ownership and commitment to the future of our community."

The conversation shifted when Paul highlighted another critical aspect, "We must also focus on healing and resilience for those directly affected by the riots. Offering support services, counseling, and resources will aid in the recovery from trauma and help pave the way for reconciliation."

Indigo spoke with a firm resolve, "By coming together as a community, listening with compassion, and aiming for shared objectives, we can begin to bridge our divides. We must commit to a future where everyone feels safe, valued, and respected. Together, we can build a resilient and peaceful Lewis Town."

The room's atmosphere subtly transformed, now tinged with a sense of purpose and a glimmer of hope.

Zach then directed the conversation towards the younger generation, "We also have to focus on our children, particularly those from Black and other minority communities. How do we equip them with hope and the tools to navigate a world deeply intertwined with interlocking social concerns?"

Hannah responded, "Our children must be prepared to face these challenges. They have to understand the systemic barriers and be empowered to overcome them. We must cultivate self-worth, resilience, and pride in their identities."

Roberta emphasized community support, "Let's make sure they know they are not alone. Building support networks and engaging with empowering communities is crucial. These connections will provide a solid foundation as they advocate for social justice and equality."

Hannah ended the meeting on a forward-looking note: "Ultimately, we are nurturing future agents of change. Our support can inspire our children to challenge injustices and strive towards a future where freedom and equality are tangible realities for everyone."

As the task force members left the room, they didn't have all the answers, but they had a more straightforward path forward and a unified commitment to fostering a more just and peaceful community. As they continued these critical conversations, their determination to support the next generation in the fight for equality and justice remained steadfast.

###

The Task Force's next meeting was held in the conference room at City Hall, and the committee members were determined to tackle the simmering tensions in Lewis Town. Hannah opened the meeting with an observation.

"The turmoil in our community isn't isolated but reflects broader societal issues we must address. I want you to consider the following question: What are the primary causes fueling this ongoing dispute?"

Indigo kicked off the talk, getting right into the thick of it. "So, the situation's pretty complex. We're looking at layers of historical land disputes and rights issues. Different groups have ideas about how to run the town, which mirrors the bigger splits we see in society."

Paul jumped in with his perspective. "And let's not forget the role of race and class here. The policies in place have hit the less privileged groups the hardest, stirring up a lot of resentment and division."

Roberta then deepened the discussion, stressing the need to look back to look forward. "If we're serious about sorting this out, we should face up to the past—how discrimination and pushing people out has shaped what's going on in Lewis Town today."

Hannah nodded, tying in more threads. "Exactly, and you can't ignore how segregation, urban development, and gentrification have worsened these divides. We've got to tackle these historical wrongs if we want to make any lasting peace."

Zach suggested a way forward. "We need a straight-up, open talk with everyone involved. We've got to develop fair solutions that tackle these deep-seated issues to start healing our community."

Building on that, Indigo pointed out a piece that often needs to be noticed. "With all the recent tension, we should listen to what women of color have to say. They bring essential perspectives that could help us figure things out."

Roberta was all for it. "Our plan must be intersectional and empowering, acknowledging their struggles and strengths."

Zach agreed, linking it to broader goals. "Bringing together race, gender, and class in our approach is key. Focusing on the needs of women of color will help us get to the heart of the issues in Lewis Town and push forward broader social justice."

Hannah concluded with a clear vision: "So, here's our mission. We're all in on boosting resilience, empowerment, and liberation. We aim for a fair and inclusive community."

Fired by their meaningful conversation, the Task Force members felt a strong sense of direction. They were laying the groundwork for tackling the challenges in Lewis Town, driven by a commitment to justice and inclusivity.

###

The next task force meeting convened in a room filled with urgency. The members were acutely aware of the community's concerns about policing and committed to exploring meaningful reform avenues. Hannah, chairing the meeting, set the tone with a clear focus on recent events.

"Colleagues, today we will explore ways law enforcement can improve their response in tension-filled scenarios to prevent exacerbating the situation and build trust within the community."

Indigo responded promptly, emphasizing the need for calm, "The police should prioritize de-escalation from the outset. Treating protesters with respect and avoiding confrontations is essential for maintaining peace."

Roberta highlighted the importance of community engagement, "Absolutely, fostering trust is paramount, and initiating open dialogues between law enforcement and the community could be beneficial. Perhaps involving community leaders and mediators early on could address the underlying causes of the unrest."

Zach focused on civil liberties, "We should ensure that law enforcement remembers that citizens have the right to protest and express their grievances. It's about striking the right balance between ensuring safety and respecting individual freedoms."

Paul emphasized the importance of oversight, "Being transparent and holding law enforcement accountable is critical. We need robust mechanisms to monitor and swiftly address misconduct or excessive force."

Hannah concluded with potential strategies, "Training our officers in de-escalation techniques, cultural sensitivity, and effective community engagement is vital. Investing in community policing strategies could significantly narrow the divide between residents and the police."

Feeling motivated, Indigo suggested specific measures: "We should advocate for policies that enhance accountability and transparency and place the community at the core of policing efforts. Addressing these issues effectively could lead to a fairer and more peaceful environment."

Roberta expressed optimism about their strategy, "I'm enthusiastic about advocating for a more compassionate and effective approach to policing."

Zach supported the collective vision, looking at the broader implications, "Let's leverage our influence to promote a policing approach that focuses on de-escalation, community engagement, and the respect of civil rights. Together, we can strive for a society where everyone feels secure, valued, and heard."

The group was unified in its mission to transform the relationship between the community and the police in Lewis Town, cultivating an atmosphere of mutual respect and understanding that could lead to enduring peace and equity.

###

Hannah initiated the next task force meeting session: "Thank you all for joining today. We will focus on our shared goal of freedom and determine how best to support one another in this mission."

Indigo responded thoughtfully, "Absolutely, Hannah. It's like we're navigating a river. Those with more resources and influence seem to sail smoothly, moving ahead quickly. These members are leading the way."

Paul nodded and added, "Right, Indigo. And then there are people in the middle, staying afloat amidst daily challenges and still pushing forward."

Roberta brought a personal touch to the discussion, "I understand, but let's also think about people like my cousin Ray. He's struggling to keep up and facing setback after setback. Every step forward seems like a battle for him."

"That's precisely why we're here," Zach interjected, acknowledging the disparity. "We recognize that not everyone experiences this journey toward freedom in the same way, nor is everyone equally equipped for it."

"It's truly disheartening," Roberta continued, "Many face huge barriers that disproportionately impact the most vulnerable among us, including widespread exclusion and discrimination. It just isn't right."

"You're spot on, Roberta," Zach agreed. "That's why we must act decisively now. We should confront these issues directly, driven by compassion and solidarity, especially for the most disadvantaged."

Looking to shift the conversation towards action, Hannah asked, "Zach, what specific steps do you think we should take first?"

"We must tackle the big systemic issues—political disenfranchisement, economic disparities, and social division. These are the real shackles for many," Zach explained. "We have to make our voices heard, ensure our votes count, and advocate for significant changes."

"And what about at the grassroots level, Zach? What strategy do you suggest there?" Indigo inquired.

"At the grassroots, it's about reaching out to those who have lost hope," Zach replied. "We must provide essentials like food and clothing and offer care to those who are ill. It's about extending a helping hand to those who feel defeated and helping to repair what's broken."

"That's a compelling vision," Paul said enthusiastically. "What if we set up subcommittees to specifically address these barriers? We could explore the root causes and find ways to overcome these challenges collectively."

"That's a fantastic idea, Paul," Hannah responded. We'll need committed volunteers to lead these subcommittees and develop actionable plans. By pooling our efforts, we can truly make a difference."

"Let's shift from discussion to action," Zach concluded. "It's time to dedicate ourselves to this work and ensure our journey leads us to the freedom we seek."

The members showed their approval and readiness to move forward.

"Thank you, everyone," Hannah concluded with a hopeful tone. "Let's proceed with determination. Let's pray, reflect, and act. Helping those in greatest need ultimately uplifts us all. Let's reconvene soon with our plans ready. May we all be blessed on this journey toward freedom."

###

Hannah listened intently as the Clerk summarized the events of the recent City Council Meeting. The Clerk gave a detailed account and informed the audience the transcript would be ready for distribution within the week. The Clerk reported that, at the last meeting, the Mayor opened the session with brief comments, salutations, and greetings to the esteemed City Council members and Lewis Town's fellow residents. Task force members Hannah and Indigo took the floor to share their insights and concerns regarding community engagement and problem-solving in our city. Their remarks shed light on crucial aspects often overlooked in our efforts for positive change.

Hannah highlighted the disconnect between community improvement discussions and the involvement of those most affected by these issues—the community members themselves. She critiqued the prevalent practice of relying on "experts" to analyze problems without adequately engaging with the residents who experience these challenges firsthand. Hannah urged deeper exploration of the root causes of neighborhood issues instead of merely debating superficial quality aspects.

In addition, Indigo stressed the importance of a holistic approach to community problem-solving. She emphasized that solutions often fail by neglecting community life's intellectual, physical, and spiritual dimensions. Indigo advocated for an inclusive strategy that values all stakeholders' diverse perspectives and wisdom, recognizing the need for a comprehensive approach to address community challenges effectively.

Both speakers underscored the necessity of precise and resident-centered community interventions for meaningful progress. They likened current efforts lacking a focused direction to "shooting arrows into the wind," highlighting the importance of purposeful and collaborative initiatives to achieve the intended outcomes.

Additionally, various community members stepped forward to share their perspectives and experiences, adding depth and diversity to the dialogue:

Concerned parents spoke passionately about safer neighborhoods and better opportunities for their children. They emphasized the importance of community resources and support systems to ensure a brighter future for the next generation.

Teenagers voiced their desire for more city youth programs, recreational facilities, and mentorship opportunities. They highlighted the importance of investing in young people to foster growth and development.

The Coalition for Women of Color shared its struggles with systemic inequalities and discrimination in Lewis Town. It called for better representation, inclusivity, and support for marginalized communities within the city.

Several White residents spoke about their commitment to allyship and solidarity with communities of color. They acknowledged their privilege and were willing to work towards a more equitable and just society.

Religious leaders emphasized the moral imperative of addressing social injustices and caring for society's most vulnerable members. They called for unity, compassion, and action rooted in shared values of love and justice.

Residents displaced by urban renewal shared their stories of displacement and loss. They highlighted the need for policies prioritizing community well-being and protecting vulnerable populations during redevelopment.

Those who historically held power and privilege in Lewis Town acknowledged their responsibility to address systemic inequities and work towards creating a more inclusive and equitable city for all residents.

The City Council meeting was transformed by the poignant and powerful testimonies of the Black mothers who had tragically lost their children to senseless violence. Standing before the council, their voices trembled with a mixture of pain, grief, and righteous anger, their eyes reflecting the weight of unbearable loss.

One mother, her voice quivering with emotion, recounted the night she received that devastating phone call informing her of her child's untimely death. Through tears and choked sobs, she shared the heart-wrenching details of the impact of that loss on her life and the lives of her family members. Her words carried the weight of a grief too profound to be adequately expressed.

Another mother, her gaze fixed on the council members, spoke with a steely resolve that belied the raw pain in her eyes. She demanded justice for her child and all the other young lives cut short by violence in the community. Her words were a call to action, a plea for accountability and systemic change to prevent further tragedies from befalling families like hers.

Each mother shared a unique story of loss, but their collective message was clear: they would not rest until their voices were heard, their pain acknowledged, and their demands for justice and change met. Their testimonies resonated with raw emotion and a fierce determination to seek accountability and reform within the community, challenging the Council and the city as a whole to confront the harsh realities of violence and its devastating impact on families.

As the room fell silent, the echoes of the words lingered, a haunting reminder of the urgent need for meaningful action and collective solidarity in addressing the deep-rooted issues of violence and injustice plaguing the community. The bravery and resilience of these mothers stood as a testament to their unwavering commitment to honoring the memories of their lost children and fighting for a future where senseless violence no longer shattered families and communities.

Each of these community members brought a unique perspective and set of experiences to the City Council meeting, enriching the dialogue and underscoring the urgent need for collective action and solidarity in addressing the pressing issues facing Lewis Town.

The consensus reached at the meeting emphasized the need for a more integrated and empathetic approach to community planning and development. Progress requires actively listening, learning from past missteps, and embracing a comprehensive strategy that considers the community's and its residents' collective well-being. Furthermore, the critical role of the church as a key stakeholder in community problem-solving was underscored, highlighting the importance of inclusive decision-making processes.

The Clerk wrapped up her summary with these words:

"As we move forward, let us heed the voices of our community members and commit to working collaboratively towards a more inclusive, equitable, and prosperous future for all residents of Lewis Town. Thank you."

###

Sitting at the wicker table in her screened-in sanctuary, Hannah enjoyed a moment of respite. The gentle sounds of the water lapping against the distant river shores filled her surroundings. The trees swayed gently in the breeze, their leaves whispering a soft caress. As she closed her eyes and listened to the symphony of nature, she sensed a call to release the burdens she carried and trust in the ebb and flow of the journey ahead. She surrendered to the current, the distant shore within her range of vision. The horizon beckoned with unknown possibilities, and as she imagined herself floating effortlessly downstream, she found a sense of liberation, allowing herself to be carried by the forces of change. In that moment of surrender, she found a renewed sense of strength and purpose, ready to continue her advocacy with a heart unburdened and a spirit renewed. Amen and Ashe.

15

2025 **The Costs of Social Change**

In their quest to breathe new life into Lewis Town, Hannah, Indigo, and Paul were mired in disheartening encounters with potential funders. Initially, they approached local business owners with a proposal for a modest increase in business and property taxes, envisioning these funds as a lifeline for essential community enhancements. With a hopeful tone, Hannah outlined how these funds would be pivotal. Yet, the response was laden with concerns; the business owners feared the immediate negative impacts amidst an unpredictable economy, worried that higher taxes might repel new investments rather than cultivate them.

Paul, sensing the mounting skepticism, tried to reassure the prospective benefactors by emphasizing the minimal nature of the increase and the long-term benefits of an improved infrastructure. However, their reassurances seemed to dissolve into the thick air of doubt that filled the room, with business owners demanding visible improvements or a phased plan that could tie tax increases to tangible community enhancements.

With spirits low, the Task Force then turned to county officials, pitching the project as a catalyst for regional development, poised to boost tourism and local commerce. The officials acknowledged the proposal's potential but delivered a blow when they revealed that the budget was already stretched thin and tied up in other infrastructure projects. They suggested that the task force reapply in the next fiscal cycle and look for alternative funding sources. This advice, though practical, felt like a polite dismissal, leaving the task force grappling with the reality of prolonged uncertainty.

Not ready to surrender, Indigo presented the project to state funding sources, framing it as a blueprint for statewide economic stability. While appreciative of the vision, the state funding officer highlighted that their current priorities were elsewhere, focusing on emergency management and health services in rural areas. They expressed an inability to fund urban redevelopment at that time. His voice tinged with desperation, Paul inquired about any upcoming grants or programs that might align with their goals, clinging to any thread of hope.

In a final attempt, the Task Force sought support from federal entities, with Paul arguing that their neighborhood improvement plan could set a national precedent for sustainable urban development. However, the federal response was discouraging; they were told that the intense competition for funds favored projects in areas of more significant socioeconomic distress.

With these continuous rejections, Indigo, Hannah, and Paul felt the heavy cloak of despair settling around them. They explored alternative funding avenues, including pitching to philanthropic organizations, considering community bonds, approaching businesses for sponsorships, and initiating a crowdfunding campaign. Each effort was met with more rejection, a relentless echo of "no" reverberating through their every attempt to move forward.

Exhausted and disheartened, the team faced the grim reality of their situation. The weight of continuous rejection pressed down on them, sapping the last reserves of their hope. They returned home, their minds clouded with the gloom of potential failure, ready to concede defeat in the face of overwhelming odds. Once so vivid and promising, the dream of revitalizing Lewis Town now seemed like a distant, fading shadow. Initially, the path to change appeared bleak, fraught with debates and skepticism. The plan's success faced substantial challenges, from overcoming the community's entrenched territorial mindset to securing the necessary funding without burdening the already taxed residents.

###

The Task Force had just about given up when, miraculously, ample funding came through as a generous donation from an anonymous benefactor.

Hannah and the team sprang into action, initiating a series of transformative initiatives designed to heal the community and address the root causes of the unrest. Each initiative was carefully deliberated to foster inclusivity, understanding, and equality across all sectors of Lewis Town.

One of the first actions would be introducing peace circles at the local community center. These gatherings would provide a safe space for residents to express their feelings, share experiences, and discuss community issues openly and without judgment. Facilitated by trained mediators, these peace circles would help break down barriers between different community groups, allowing empathy and understanding to grow.

Recognizing the need for reform in law enforcement practices, the task force planned to establish coalitions between the police and the community. These coalitions would build trust and cooperation through regular meetings, joint community projects, and officer participation in community events. Officers would receive training in de-escalation techniques, cultural competency, and community policing strategies, which would be instrumental in reshaping the relationship between law enforcement and the residents they serve.

Efforts to uplift economically disadvantaged residents would be significantly enhanced. The task force would get funding for educational and vocational training programs, financial literacy workshops, and job placement services. These initiatives would provide the tools and opportunities necessary for upward mobility, thereby addressing one of the root causes of the community's tensions.

Recognizing the psychological impact of the riots and ongoing socioeconomic stresses, the task force would increase the number of counselors available in schools, community centers, and clinics. These professionals would provide critical support, helping individuals and families navigate their trauma and fostering a healthier community environment.

A new field house would be built to promote community cohesion and provide a venue for recreational and social activities. This facility would include spaces for sports, community meetings, and youth programs, serving as a hub for engagement and positive interactions among residents of all ages.

To address socioeconomic and racial disparities in housing, the Rivercrest Senior Living Center, previously an exclusive enclave for the wealthy, would be expanded to include residents from all races and income levels.

This initiative would provide quality living conditions for more seniors and foster a more diverse and inclusive community environment.

###

The Task Force further tapped into regional, state, and federal grants. Their efforts began to crystallize in visible changes in the landscape and spirit of Lewis Town. One of the earliest and most notable improvement projects was the expansion of Riverfront Park, sponsored by a philanthropic organization dedicated to enhancing the city's communal spaces. This expanded park became a beacon of communal interaction, promoting environmental appreciation and social gatherings. The intersection of Independence Boulevard and Jordan Avenue was another focal point of redevelopment. It underwent significant refurbishment, which included the construction of historical landmarks and a museum dedicated to preserving and celebrating Lewis Town's history. These developments served as a nod to the past and a commitment to the town's future.

However, the transformation process had its challenges. Some longtime residents, tired of the ongoing changes and continuous construction, chose to relocate in search of quieter surroundings. This demographic shift gradually increased the community's average age, highlighting a growing need to support its aging population.

Additional projects initiated in Lewis Town marked significant steps toward community renewal and restoration. These changes not only revitalized physical spaces but also mended the social fabric of a once-divided community, steering it toward a future of unity and mutual respect. Through these initiatives, the Lewis Town Task Force for Change began to mend the deep wounds inflicted by the unrest and longstanding issues within the community. Each step forward was a testament to the town's resilience and commitment to creating a fair, just, and unified community for all its residents.

###

Now that the hard work was done, Hannah and Indigo decided to spend a lazy Saturday afternoon nibbling on the peach cobbler Indigo had brought to Hannah's house. Hannah provided the coffee and an idyllic place to sit as they enjoyed the sights and sounds of the river in the distance. Sitting on Hannah's cozy screened-in porch, the two friends sipped their coffee, basking in the comfort of their shared sisterhood.

The pivotal role of Black female pastors in the struggle for change was heavy on Hannah's heart. While organizing, Hannah interacted with many pastors she met on the march for justice. Most of these leaders stood in solidarity with a spokesperson they had selected to represent them at a public podium. Others used their churches as sanctuaries and meeting places for organizing and debriefing. They all desired social change, but few were Black females.

Hannah reflected on the unique perspective, sensitivity, and leadership style she brought to her ministry, emphasizing how vital these qualities were in meeting Black women's spiritual, emotional, and social needs in her congregation. She tried her best to foster inclusivity, empathy, empowerment, and community. She was dedicated to nurturing a supportive environment that resonated deeply with the people she encountered.

Deep in thought, Hannah opened up to Indigo, her trusted confidant, about her role within her community as a Black female pastor.

"There's something powerful about being in this position," Hannah reflected. "When people see someone who looks like them, who understands their struggles and dreams, it sparks a fire in them to envision themselves in roles of influence and leadership."

Hannah explained how her identity as a woman shaped her pastoral approach, infusing her caregiving with empathy and sensitivity.

"When I look at the people I serve, I can say I've been where they are. Our shared understanding creates space for deep empathy and nurturing," Hannah said.

Addressing the gender-specific challenges faced by many Black women, Hannah spoke of creating a safe space for difficult conversations around gender discrimination, sexism, and issues like domestic violence and reproductive health.

"These are not just topics; I lived through and observed the same experiences as those who seek me for spiritual care," she emphasized.

Hannah cultivated a sense of sisterhood and community central to her mission. "It goes beyond Sunday services," she elaborated. "It's about building connections that uplift and empower. I'm always seeking ways for Black women to unite, share their stories, and strengthen each other. This sisterhood is a wellspring of strength and a guiding light for spiritual and personal growth."

"You have a caring heart and a giving spirit," Indigo attested. "Because you're a woman and an experienced leader with a deep toolkit, you can advocate for gender equality and social justice. By standing in your pulpit, you're saying that leadership and authority are not limited by gender," Indigo asserted.

"I also think I'm a mentor," Hannah added. "Mentoring is about guiding, encouraging, and inspiring," she said warmly. "It's about helping the next generation discover and follow their unique spiritual paths. I'm here to lead and walk alongside them on their journey."

"I agree with you, " Indigo said. "As a female pastor to Black women, your responsibilities go beyond the traditional pastoral duties. You have to be a leader, a friend, an advocate, and a sister in faith," she concluded with unwavering resolve.

"It's a role I embrace wholeheartedly, and I am fully aware of its profound impact," Hannah concluded.

###

The entire community gathered at the new Lewis Town Memorial Field House. Its sleek, modern lines stood in beautiful contrast to the natural surroundings. The large windows of the gym and pool areas offered panoramic views of the river, allowing sunlight to play across the water's surface. The elegantly curved concert shell added a sophisticated touch to the structure, enhancing the scenic riverfront. Onlookers admired the seamless integration of contemporary architecture with the pristine beauty of the riverfront. The atmosphere was both solemn and hopeful.

The dedication of the new field house on the riverfront was a landmark event. The atmosphere was electric with excitement and anticipation. The ceremony started with Hannah's invocation, setting a peaceful and upbeat tone for the occasion. Paul shared heartfelt insights into the tireless efforts and dedication that brought the field house project to fruition. Indigo arranged for the local high school band to provide music, adding to the celebratory atmosphere.

This event marked the opening of a new communal space and symbolized the town's ongoing efforts to heal and grow together. During the ceremony, a series of plaques were unveiled. These plaques commemorated the lives and legacies of people who inspired the community's path toward unity and healing and detailed its historical development. This act of remembrance emphasized the community's commitment to acknowledging its past while building toward a more inclusive and harmonious future.

###

Following the program, guests gathered for the celebratory picnic. The sun cast a warm, inviting glow over the park, beckoning everyone to join the festivities. Even the most reserved among the community residents stepped out to mingle and participate in the joyous occasion.

Hannah opened the picnic with remarks. Her words echoed through the park, setting the tone for a day of celebration and reflection. The sights and sounds of gladness and togetherness enveloped the community at the festivities.

"Good afternoon, everyone," Hannah said with joy. "As we gather here today to celebrate this occasion, I want to take a moment to reflect on its significance in the context of our community's efforts to restore peace and cooperation in Lewis Town. This celebration is vital to our community's commitment to unity and reconciliation. This event has the potential to bridge divides, promote understanding, and foster solidarity among all residents. Today, as we come together, let us use this opportunity for education, dialogue, reflecting on the legacy of slavery, racism, and discrimination in America, but looking forward to a new day. Through cultural events, historical exhibits, and community gatherings, we can learn about past challenges, celebrate progress, and collectively work towards a more inclusive and equitable future for all. Let us embrace freedom, justice, and unity as we strengthen our bonds, cultivate empathy and respect, and create a more harmonious and cooperative environment for every community member. Let us allow the celebration to serve as a powerful catalyst for positive change, healing, and reconciliation as we continue on our journey toward a future of peace, cooperation, and mutual understanding. Enjoy the day. Thank you."

On one end of the park, people were engaged in a spirited game of lawn polo, their laughter mingling with the gentle clinks of mallets striking balls through wire hoops. Nearby, the tranquility of Tai Chi sessions offered a soothing contrast as participants moved gracefully in sync. For those who preferred a bit of strategy and mental challenge, tables were laden with Scrabble boards, jigsaw puzzles, and bingo cards, drawing in newcomers and seasoned players alike. The highlight, however, was the Uno game, where Jonathan, Myrtle, Janet, and William were locked in a friendly but fierce battle. Cheers erupted when William, with a triumphant grin, declared, "Uno!" while expertly balancing his cane. The committee outdid itself with a delightful spread of boxed lunches featuring sandwiches, fresh fruit, and chips, ensuring no one went hungry. The highlight was the hand-churned ice cream station, where everyone savored the rich, creamy flavors made right in the local deli.

Throughout the day, the festivities provided moments of fun and enjoyment. They reinforced the bonds of camaraderie and support that define the community, showcasing the resilience and spirit of togetherness that unite residents in their shared journey toward peace, cooperation, and mutual understanding. As the day transitioned to evening, residents spread their blankets and prepared for the grand finale. As the first firework shot into the sky, a collective gasp of wonder rose from the crowd. The night sky became a canvas, painted with vibrant bursts of color that reflected on the awed faces of the community members. The symphony of light and sound enveloped everyone, weaving a backdrop for unity.

###

Hannah sat quietly on her porch. The mighty river flowed steadily just a short distance away, its calm waters mirroring her longing for balance in the currents of life. Hannah grew aware that her chosen path was formidable, akin to her ancestors' journey toward the hopeful yet distant shores of freedom. Hannah's endeavors to rejuvenate the town, infusing life into every brick and street, were a testament to her courage and love for her community.

In her mind's eye, Hannah imagined her community as travelers on a mighty river. Some navigated the currents effortlessly, reaching great heights, while the steady voyagers, the heart and soul of the town, pushed forward with relentless hope. Then, some faced hardships unknown to others who rode smoother waters. Hannah felt a warmth, like the gentle squeeze of a hand, as she considered these images. The community was finally on a course for transformation. The journey would be long, and the river winding, but together, they would discover ways to navigate the mighty waters, reaching back to ensure that others did not drown. Amen and Ashe.

16

2028 **Rivercrest Senior Living**

Through a strategic grant, existing nursing facilities were consolidated into a new establishment named Rivercrest Senior Living Center. Built on a site previously demolished by urban renewal, this facility was designed to provide a continuum of care for older people. Set near the scenic Grandview River, Rivercrest Center offered its residents various options—from independent living in single-family cottages to assisted living, memory care, and hospice services.

The center, boasting fifteen acres of lush landscapes with towering trees and cooling breezes from the nearby river, quickly became known for its peaceful environment and comprehensive care. Recognizing the changing demographics and the importance of inclusivity, Rivercrest Center expanded its admission criteria to include a more racially and economically diverse population. This decision was rooted in a commitment to social justice and equity, aiming to reflect the diversity of the broader world within its community. The inclusive policy fostered an enriching environment where cultural exchanges and diverse experiences thrived, enhancing the quality of life for all residents. The community at Rivercrest Center tailored its services and programs to meet the diverse needs of its inhabitants, from cultural festivities to diverse culinary offerings and specialized healthcare services. Rivercrest Center became more than just a place to live; it embodied the values of fairness, respect, and social responsibility. It stood as a testament to the town's dedication to creating a just and vibrant environment for all its residents.

###

The evolution of residential living for senior citizens is worthy of note. These centers were ingeniously crafted to accommodate the diverse needs of seniors through various stages of their lives—from independent living to assisted living, skilled nursing, memory care, and hospice services. This model facilitated a smooth transition between care levels as residents' needs evolved, fostering a stable and connected community environment that resonated with hope and continuity.

In earlier times, these comprehensive care facilities were essentially the privilege of those with considerable financial means. Steep entry fees and costly monthly rates barred many, particularly individuals from lower socioeconomic backgrounds and various racial and ethnic groups, from accessing these essential services.

However, change was sparked as societal consciousness about equity in elder care grew. Advocates for older people and champions of social justice called attention to the stark disparities in access to quality senior care based on income and ethnicity. They pushed for inclusive and equitable models.

The tide began to turn in recent years, thanks to a collective push to democratize access to these pivotal services. Governments at multiple levels stepped forward, implementing policies to promote fairness in senior care access. This included subsidies, grants, and changes to zoning laws that encouraged the development of affordable senior housing options. Partnerships between local governments, private developers, and nonprofit organizations flourished, aiming to construct and manage affordable senior living centers.

Communities, too, played their part, rallying behind local nonprofits focused on senior care or initiating community-funded affordable living options. The growing awareness of the need for equitable senior living solutions also caught the attention of philanthropists and foundations, whose contributions furthered the development of financially accessible senior living models.

As these centers evolved, they began to reflect holistic approaches that addressed not only the physical health of seniors but also their mental, emotional, and social well-being. This shift influenced the design of centers to be culturally inclusive and supportive, ensuring that every resident felt valued and respected.

This transformation brought about numerous benefits. Residents from diverse racial, ethnic, and economic backgrounds could now enjoy a life of dignity in settings that respected their cultural preferences and needs. These centers became melting pots of diversity, fostering broad social support networks that were vital for the mental and emotional health of the residents.

Thus, the movement toward inclusive residential senior living centers marked a pivotal chapter in ensuring that all seniors, regardless of their financial situation or background, received the care and support they needed in their twilight years. This progressive approach enhanced the quality of life for older people and enriched the very fabric of their communities, creating environments brimming with diversity and mutual support.

###

Denise tried to contain her excitement during her orientation for the activities director position at the Rivercrest Senior Living Center. The center embraced a Montessori approach to address older adults' unique challenges. Its programs fostered individualized learning, independence, hands-on experiences, physical engagement, cognitive stimulation, and emotional connection. The activities director would coordinate activities across residential, assisted living, and memory-care units and occasionally help with worship services and special programs. Denise accepted the job.

Rivercrest already boasted a well-defined fitness program. Their routine included seventy-five to 150 minutes per week of moderate-intensity activities such as walking, hiking, jogging, biking, and dancing, along with muscle-strengthening and balance-improvement exercises twice weekly. These activities were carefully adjusted to accommodate health conditions common in those over sixty-five, such as osteoporosis, cardiovascular disease, obesity, and arthritis.

The program also featured games to enhance socialization and stimulate cognitive functions. Activity lounges offered a variety of board games, card games, puzzles, and memory games, with bingo being a particular favorite among the community. Reading, listening to audiobooks, arts and crafts, and storytelling sessions were actively promoted. Residents could also enjoy the beautiful Rivercrest campus outdoors, engaging in bird watching, nature walks, or simply relaxing on scenic porches or balconies. Denise had already scheduled a meeting with the Program Planning Committee to finalize plans for the upcoming 4th of July festivities.

As Denise contemplated the scope of her role, she envisioned the activities she might organize. Recognizing the importance of catering to individual learning styles, she considered incorporating arts and crafts, gardening, cooking, and memory games. Her goal was to engage multiple senses—touch, sight, smell, and sound—to evoke memories, provide comfort, and promote emotional well-being. She planned to create environments with clear signage, organized spaces, and consistent routines to ensure residents felt secure. She also considered including cultural celebrations, exercise classes for various fitness levels, and a diverse menu. She aimed to address all residents' emotional, physical, intellectual, and spiritual well-being, regardless of their background, physical abilities, or age. She aspired to foster a nurturing community among this diverse group.

###

On her first day at work, Denise received a grand tour. The campus manager proudly showcased the meticulously manicured grounds. "Our groundskeepers take great pride in maintaining the campus," he explained as they toured the facility.

"It is stunning," Denise responded, admiring the cozy seating arrangements and spectacular views.

The campus manager also highlighted the effective maintenance routines, particularly during winter, sharing an anecdote about assisting a resident who had slipped on ice, underscoring the staff's attentiveness to safety and care.

"This is a huge campus," Denise noted as they continued the tour.

The main building housed administrative offices, a waiting room with a grand piano, a gift shop, banquet rooms, and a restaurant and deli for the residents. The chapel was conveniently located in the main building next to the offices for Spiritual Care. An intricate series of underground tunnels connected all the campus buildings, ensuring easy and comfortable movement regardless of weather conditions. A parking lot for residents with cars and a shuttle bus service for non-drivers enhanced mobility for errands on designated days.

As Denise and the campus manager walked along the winding pathways, they were greeted by vibrant flower gardens that bloomed in a riot of colors throughout the seasons. Water fountains dotted the landscape, providing the soothing sound of running water and creating a tranquil atmosphere for residents to relax and unwind. Seating areas were strategically placed throughout the community, allowing residents to sit and enjoy the river view. They paused momentarily to catch their breath, taking in the serene and picturesque environment that Denise would now be a part of, contributing to the richness of life at Rivercrest Senior Living Center.

###

During her initial weeks at Rivercrest Center, Denise visited the activities center to evaluate its potential. The lounge was a cozy and inviting space where residents could relax and socialize. Tables were ideally suited for playing games or assembling puzzles, while the sofas offered comfortable seating for watching TV or conversing with friends. Various stations were well-stocked with activities catering to different interests, ranging from the excitement of bingo to the creativity of knitting. A fully equipped kitchen was an excellent resource for residents who enjoyed cooking and hosting gatherings. Large picture windows framed a beautiful river view, enhancing the scenic ambiance of the lounge.

Despite their advancing years, a group of dedicated residents regularly made their way to the gym in matching workout gear on Tuesdays and Thursdays. Denise confidently led this group, her slightly graying hair and the familiar twinkle in her eye signaling her leadership. They typically began with light dumbbell curls, demonstrating their strength and determination. Meanwhile, greeting her with warm smiles and youthful energy, other residents headed to the treadmill. This group set the machines to a moderate pace and slowly walked, pushing themselves as far as possible.

As the residents moved through their workout routine, they encouraged, supported, and challenged each other to push harder, lift heavier, and run faster, affirming that age is merely a number for maintaining fitness and health. After their workout, they cooled down together, stretching, rehydrating, and discussing the day's events. They usually left the gym feeling invigorated and proud of their achievements.

In planning activities for the residents at Rivercrest Senior Living, Denise considered a diverse range of options that catered to all age groups and capacity levels. At the heart of Rivercrest's wellness offerings were low-impact exercise classes such as chair yoga, Tai Chi, and gentle stretching, specially adapted for those with mobility or physical limitations. These activities were designed not just for physical movement but to enhance the overall well-being of the community's seniors.

Rivercrest's arts and crafts sessions encouraged creativity, offering painting, drawing, pottery, and scrapbooking. These activities, tailored to different skill levels and incorporating adaptive tools, allowed everyone to engage regardless of their abilities. Music therapy sessions utilized the soothing power of music through singing, instrument playing, and group music activities, which are known for their therapeutic and mood-enhancing effects.

Intergenerational programs at Rivercrest bridged gaps through activities like reading circles, storytelling, art projects, and gardening, fostering social interaction and mutual support across different age groups. The joys of gardening were embraced in the facility's garden spaces, where residents could plant flowers, herbs, or vegetables, connecting with nature and reaping physical, cognitive, and sensory benefits.

Educational enrichment was ongoing through lectures, discussion groups, book clubs, and trivia games, inviting guest speakers and experts to lead sessions as engaging as they were informative. Pet therapy sessions brought the therapeutic presence of animals to the facility, offering comfort and companionship that helped reduce stress and improve mood among residents. Culinary interests were catered to through cooking demonstrations, baking classes, and culinary workshops, where residents learned new recipes and techniques with hands-on participation. Mindfulness and meditation were also integral, with programs promoting mental clarity, stress reduction, and emotional well-being. Social activities at Rivercrest included themed parties, holiday celebrations, and group outings vital for building friendships and community engagement, creating an inclusive atmosphere where every resident felt valued and connected.

At Rivercrest Center, each program and activity was more than just a pastime; they were bridges to a fuller, more vibrant life for every resident, ensuring their days were filled with growth, joy, and a sense of belonging. Through offering diverse activities tailored to individual needs, Denise promoted the residents' physical, mental, emotional, and social well-being, fostering a vibrant and engaging environment for all.

###

Denise encountered Susan, one of the White residents, at a table in the shared lounge one day. Susan had grown up on the north side of Lewis Town near the river. As Denise approached, Susan waved and smiled warmly.

"How are you today? Did you enjoy the movie yesterday?" Denise asked.

"I sure did. Have a seat," Susan invited, gesturing to a chair beside her. Denise sat down. "Great action. I love action flicks."

As they conversed, Denise learned that Susan enjoyed engaging with anyone willing to listen. It soon became evident to Denise that Susan had thrived in various careers and had traveled extensively.

"I'm moving tomorrow," Susan revealed after a pause.

"Where are you going?" Denise inquired.

"It's on the second floor, right above where we're seated, in Room 214. I don't know if that's a promotion or a demotion!" Susan joked.

"Why are you moving?" Denise asked.

"There are more people around. I like to play bridge, so there might be more people to play with. There are more people to talk to."

A brief silence fell between them.

"My brother called to wish me luck with the move. You know, he's building a home in South Carolina. It's going to have handicapped access, with ramps and all. I'm going to pay 50 percent of the cost of the home. I guess I'll own half of it. I don't mind. He wants me to try it out for a short time first. And if it doesn't work out, there's a residential home in Charlottesville. I could live there."

"Is it like this one?"

"Yes, I think so. I don't want to be a burden to anyone. If he and his current wife want to spend time together, I don't want to stop them. I don't want them to have to worry about me."

Denise acknowledged her words with a slight nod. Again, there was a comfortable silence for a few seconds.

"Where were you born?" Denise asked.

"Lewis Town. Just up the road a bit," Susan responded.

"It's a small world!" Denise remarked. "My mother was born there, too."

"I remember we used to go to Riverview in the city," Susan said. "The House of Mirrors was one of my favorite attractions with all those distorted figures. And I liked the Bobs. And the Fireball! I remember that after riding the roller coaster, you could pay twenty-five cents to ride again. You could ride all day if you wanted to. I also liked the water shoots," Susan said.

The grin on Susan's face demonstrated the joy of her experiences. She continued her remembrances.

"Another thing I liked to do was bike. One year, two other people and I biked all over Europe, going through England, France, and Italy."

"How long were you there?" Denise asked.

"Eleven weeks. We rode a little, hiked a little, and did some sightseeing—that kind of thing. Sometimes, we hitchhiked when we were in the mountains. We'd load our bikes in the back of the truck. They always made me sit in the middle near the driver. I didn't like that so much because the truck drivers used to reach over and squeeze my knees. I didn't like that! Once, the truck driver got out to pump some gas, and I told the others that they would have to take turns sitting in the middle. So, we switched off after that. The tour company was excellent, and the cost was reasonable. Three bikes for eleven weeks was only about $1200 altogether."

"That seems reasonable!" Denise exclaimed.

"I've taken some great trips to Thailand, Alsace, India. We also went to Iceland and Canada. Have you ever been?"

"No, I haven't," Denise replied.

###

For a change of pace, Denise invited her mother, Hannah, to join her for lunch at the bustling employee cafeteria at Rivercrest. Given their demanding schedules, they had rarely enjoyed the time to sit down together and talk. However, they shared a table today, with Denise eager to discuss her new role.

Denise broached the subject, occupying her thoughts as they settled into their seats. "I've been looking into the variety of senior living options offered at Rivercrest, from independent to assisted living. It's quite intriguing to see how each level of care differs," she remarked, stirring her coffee thoughtfully.

Hannah nodded, understanding the topic's importance. "Independent living communities are ideal for still active seniors who prefer to manage their daily routines without assistance. The communities provide numerous amenities and activities that support an active, independent lifestyle," she explained.

Denise, always keen to grasp the subtleties, added, "Yes, and these amenities often include meals, housekeeping, and transportation, which help residents maintain a hassle-free life. It's all about promoting wellness and social interaction."

"Exactly," Hannah agreed. "Also, assisted living offers more support. It's designed for seniors who need extra help with everyday activities like dressing, eating, or managing medications."

Denise reflected on this and said, "Assisted living facilities also provide personal care and ensure staff members are trained to support the residents' needs. They offer social activities and amenities similar to independent living but with added assistance."

Hannah leaned in slightly, emphasizing their next point. "Right, and the two differ in terms of medical care. In independent living, residents typically handle their healthcare arrangements. They're pretty much on their own when managing appointments or treatments."

"In assisted living," Denise continued, "some level of medical support, like medication management and health monitoring, is available, which can be crucial for those who might not be able to handle these responsibilities alone."

"And then there's the cost factor," Hannah pointed out. "Independent living tends to be less expensive since it doesn't include personal care services. The costs generally cover the rent and possibly additional fees for specific amenities."

"Assisted living, though more costly, includes a comprehensive package that covers room and board, along with the personal care services and amenities, reflecting the higher level of care and support provided," Denise added, summarizing the financial implications.

Hannah smiled, considering the options they had discussed. "It's really about matching the senior's needs with the right environment, whether they value independence or need more comprehensive support."

"Absolutely," Denise agreed wholeheartedly. "Understanding the options helps us guide individuals and families to make the best choices for their circumstances and needs. It's all about enhancing their quality of life at different stages."

Denise concluded. "Maybe one day, you and Dad would consider living here."

###

Hannah reclined thoughtfully on the chaise lounge on her porch. She found herself in a contemplative state, her attention drawn to the life cycle of the leaves through the changing seasons. With their continuous cycle of birth, life, decay, and rebirth, these leaves offered a profound reflection of human experiences, revealing the visible and invisible processes that carry deeper meanings akin to the chapters of one's life. Hannah contemplated the passing of the seasons.

Spring marked a delicate awakening, much like the world emerging from a long slumber. The barren branches began to show signs of vitality, with tiny buds swelling and bursting into small, tender leaves. These vibrant green leaves, almost translucent in their freshness, were eager to absorb the sun's rays, initiating their cycle of growth and photosynthesis. This season of renewal and immense growth was reminiscent of youth, filled with potential and the eagerness to explore.

As the days lengthened and the sun climbed higher, the leaves matured into their full vigor. They expanded, robust, and broad, forming a dense canopy that danced in the summer breeze. These leaves, now vigorous workhorses, engaged in photosynthesis at total capacity, converting sunlight into energy that fed the tree, supported its growth, and sustained life around it. This season mirrored the periods of our lives when we were most productive and energetic.

Then, a spectacular transformation occurred as the air cooled and the days shortened. The green leaves faded, unveiling brilliant shades of yellow, orange, red, and eventually brown. This change, prompted by the breakdown of chlorophyll, revealed the pigments previously hidden, showcasing a final glorious display before the leaves detached and drifted to the ground. This autumnal phase echoed the later stages of life, where true colors and accumulated wisdom were proudly displayed before moving into a quieter, introspective period.

With winter's arrival, the trees stood bare, their fallen leaves carpeting the earth below, where they decomposed and enriched the soil. This quiet, unseen process prepared the ground for future growth. Now conserving its energy, the tree focused on survival, awaiting the cycle to begin anew. This season of dormancy spoke to the essential times of rest and reflection in our lives, necessary for rejuvenation and continued growth.

This continual cycle of the leaves resonated deeply with Hannah, striking a chord with her journey through life. Each growth, maturity, and decline phase came with the promise of renewal. Just as the leaves adapted to the challenges posed by their environment, they offered a powerful metaphor for embracing each season of life with grace and anticipation. Hannah was inspired to learn from the silent wisdom of the leaves, to embrace each changing season of her life just as the tree gracefully accepted each shift in the year. Amen and Ashe.

17

2029 The Chapel

Rivercrest Senior Living Center was looking for a chaplain to join their team, a role that intrigued Hannah. She leaned back in her chair and contemplated the recent offer from Rivercrest to work as a chaplain there. Working in a senior living center would starkly contrast to the bustling corridors of the hospital where she once served as a chaplain. The memories of that time were vivid in her mind—long shifts, the echo of urgent footsteps, the deep spiritual conversations held beside hospital beds. It had been demanding but profoundly fulfilling work.

Chaplains at Rivercrest were integral to the fabric of daily life, providing spiritual support across a spectrum of religious and personal backgrounds. They organized and led religious services ranging from prayer groups and Bible studies to inclusive interfaith ceremonies. This aspect reminded Hannah of her hospital days when she tailored spiritual care to suit the individual beliefs of patients and staff, fostering an environment of respect and inclusion. However, at Rivercrest, the scope of pastoral care seemed even broader. One-on-one pastoral counseling was a significant part of the job, offering residents a compassionate ear during life transitions, health declines, or personal losses. Hannah remembered similar encounters in the hospital, where the immediacy of crisis often brought these issues to the forefront more abruptly.

Moreover, the chaplain's role at Rivercrest extended to supporting the families of residents, helping them navigate the emotional and spiritual complexities of aging, illness, and grief. This was somewhat different from her hospital role, where family interactions were often brief and occurred under acute stress. At Rivercrest, there seemed to be a more significant opportunity for ongoing support and more profound relationship building. The chaplain's input at Rivercrest was crucial in care team meetings, ensuring that residents' spiritual and emotional needs were considered alongside their physical health. Hannah had always advocated for this holistic approach in the hospital, often in a more crisis-driven context. The environment at Rivercrest also required a continuous presence of empathy and advocacy, promoting a sense of community and belonging. Hannah knew the value of this well; the sense of community could be a powerful healing force, just as it had been in her previous role.

As Hannah mulled over these responsibilities, she realized that while the settings might differ—the serene halls of Rivercrest versus the urgent, clinical pathways of the hospital—the core of the chaplaincy was much the same. It was about providing spiritual and emotional sanctuary, guiding through crises, and enhancing the lives of those she served through compassionate and spiritual leadership. The transition would surely bring new challenges, but it also promised new rewards—more profound relationships, a more stable environment, and the chance to weave spiritual well-being into the everyday tapestry of life in ways she had always hoped.

###

Peggy, a vibrant young redhead with a rosy complexion, guided Hannah through the Spiritual Care Department. Hannah found Peggy's understanding of community dynamics enlightening. It was evident to Hannah that Peggy was passionate about fostering a welcoming and inclusive atmosphere. Hannah recognized Peggy as an invaluable member of the Spiritual Care Department and anticipated that she would provide excellent support and guidance as Hannah acclimated to her new role.

As Peggy and Hannah settled into the quiet embrace of the chapel, Peggy shared her thoughts on the space with gentle enthusiasm. "This chapel," she began, "serves as a sanctuary of serenity and beauty. It's a haven where individuals find inner peace and connect with something greater than themselves." She elaborated on its role in fostering deep contemplation and reflection, her voice imbuing the air with a reverence for the place.

Absorbing the tranquil atmosphere, Hannah felt a soothing reprieve from the relentless pace of the external world. As they sat there, the stained-glass windows caught her eye. These vibrant panes, illustrating scenes from religious texts, bathed the chapel in a kaleidoscope of light, enhancing the sense of peace.

Hannah pointed to the piano and organ at the front of the chapel. "It's wonderful that you have both a piano and organ here," she remarked.

Peggy smiled, nodding in agreement. "Yes, they are well-used. Guest musicians often grace us with their talents during services and special events," she explained. She gestured towards the choir loft, adding, "We also host holiday concerts here. During Easter, for instance, a group of residents performs a cantata. It's truly moving how the music fills the space, enveloping everyone in sound."

Their conversation, marked by warmth and mutual appreciation for the chapel's offerings, deepened their understanding of the sanctuary as a place of worship, community, and artistic expression.

###

As Hannah settled into her new role, she visited Peggy's office often. The morning light filtered in, casting a warm glow that matched the tone of their conversation.

"Good morning, Peggy," Hannah began. "I was thinking about the chapel. What types of daily services and activities do we typically host there?"

Peggy explained. "We hold regular religious services, worship gatherings, and prayer meetings, all led by a dedicated team of chaplains, clergy, and volunteers. Beyond traditional rituals, we offer meditation classes, mindfulness sessions, inspirational talks, and music performances. It's about fostering spiritual growth and community engagement through diverse activities."

Hannah nodded, clearly impressed. "I appreciate how inclusive the chapel is. How do we ensure we meet all residents' spiritual needs, regardless of their faith backgrounds?"

"Inclusivity is at the heart of our mission," Peggy affirmed. "The chapel is a safe, supportive space for everyone to explore their spirituality and practice their beliefs. We provide various resources and pastoral care services, including counseling and grief support, to address the holistic well-being of our residents."

Hannah's voice was filled with gratitude. "Thank you for explaining the details. For many, it is a place of comfort, inspiration, and peace."

Peggy smiled. "If you have any questions, my door is always open."

###

Months later, Hannah met Wilma Lee, who had been navigating the challenges of the medical unit at Rivercrest. Walking into Wilma Lee's room, Hannah found the lights dimmed, with Wilma Lee resting in the bed near the window. The room showed signs of Wilma Lee's ongoing struggle, with unfinished meals on the bedside tray and her appearance slightly unkempt. Wilma Lee was on the phone, quickly wrapping up the call by saying she would talk later because "the chaplain is here." She then beckoned Hannah to come closer.

"Hi, my name is Hannah. Are you Wilma Lee?" Hannah asked gently.

"Yes. That was my brother on the phone," Wilma Lee replied, her voice weary yet relieved. "I'm glad you came by."

"What's been happening?" Hannah inquired, her tone soft and inviting.

"I am overwhelmed! I've been awake since 4 a.m. There's always something—blood work, vitals, wound care, doctor visits. It's been nonstop," Wilma Lee confessed, her frustration evident.

"I'm sorry to hear that you're feeling this way," Hannah responded empathetically, setting aside her clipboard to give Wilma Lee her full attention.

"I've been in medical care for three months. Today's the first day I've managed to get dressed," Wilma Lee said in a voice that was a mix of pride and disappointment.

Hannah nodded, encouraging Wilma Lee to continue.

"I went to physical therapy today but was too tired to meet my goals. I didn't accomplish anything I wanted to do," Wilma Lee continued, tears forming.

"What were your goals?" Hannah asked, her voice calm and encouraging.

"I was supposed to do some upper body exercises and walk around a bit. But I didn't make it to the bathroom in time, and it was too much," Wilma Lee admitted, reaching for a tissue.

Wilma Lee paused, wiping her tears before adding, "But I've been praying. I have faith that God will bring me through this."

"Let's look at your progress," Hannah suggested gently. "You are out of intensive care, you're dressed, and your wounds are healing. You're making small steps toward better health every day, right?"

After a reflective pause, Wilma Lee nodded. "I hadn't looked at it that way. I'm focusing too much on the negatives. I've lost significant weight since I arrived, and I can now use a standard wheelchair."

"That's incredible progress, Wilma Lee. And you have the support of your family, too. That's also something to be thankful for," Hannah affirmed, lifting Wilma Lee's spirits.

Wilma Lee smiled, a glimmer of hope in her eyes. "You're right. Thank you," she said, her mood visibly brighter. Then, inspired, she began to sing, "Walk in the light, beautiful light."

Moved by the moment, Hannah joined in, their voices blending harmoniously. The song filled the room, lifting both of their spirits.

"That was amazing," Hannah complimented Wilma Lee afterward. "I heard you were the lead singer in a world-renowned choir."

Wilma Lee beamed with pride. "Yes, we traveled the world singing. It's a blessing to remember those times."

"Indeed, it is," Hannah acknowledged, her heart warmed by the interaction. "Just take it one day at a time, Wilma Lee. You are moving forward, and that's what counts."

"You have been such a blessing today," Wilma Lee said, her expression grateful. "Thank you for helping me see my progress."

"It has been my pleasure," Hannah replied, her spirit uplifted by the encounter. "Have a good night."

As Hannah left the room, she felt a sense of peace, knowing Wilma Lee was rediscovering her strength and faith through their shared moment of music and reflection. Hannah carried this joy with her, feeling a profound connection to the power of empathetic support and the healing nature of music.

###

Hannah and Peggy had chosen one of the benches outside the chapel as the setting for their conversation. It was a peaceful spot, ideal for the kind of thoughtful discussion that was unfolding between them. As the spiritual care director, Peggy was well-versed in the dynamics of the Rivercrest community and was eager to share her insights with Hannah.

"Our residents come from various parts of the state," Peggy began, her voice reflecting a mix of pride and responsibility. "Before retiring, many held significant roles in the corporate world. Now, they channel that experience into leading and participating in various committees here at Rivercrest."

Hannah, intrigued, leaned in slightly. "What kind of committees?" she asked, genuinely interested in how such accomplished individuals contributed to the community.

"There are several," Peggy responded, her eyes lighting up. "One committee organizes projects like beautifying our main entryway with weekly floral arrangements. Another committee also plans annual outings to Ravinia for those who enjoy concerts. Often, these groups invite another chaplain or me to open their meetings with an invocation. They also seek our input on various matters. You'll meet them soon, and they'll benefit from your expertise in planning upcoming activities."

Hannah nodded, absorbing the information. "It sounds like considerable diversity is here," she remarked, holding back a personal anecdote about her encounters in Lewis Town.

"That's correct," Peggy agreed. "The community initially started as a denominational initiative to provide a secure environment for parishioners in their retirement years. We significantly expanded a decade ago thanks to a grant from a generous benefactor. The residents are learning to coexist in what I'd call an off-key harmony."

"That sounds promising," Hannah commented, her tone optimistic yet contemplative.

Peggy nodded, her expression becoming slightly more serious. "It is, but it's important to recognize the social dynamics here. There's a distinct hierarchy among the residents. At the top are the old-guard elites with their traditional ways of thinking and living. Conversely, we have those who are either too old or ill to engage in community politics. Then there's a large group of newcomers in the middle, bringing varied cultures, classes, and religious backgrounds."

"Planning activities for such a diverse group must present some challenges," Hannah observed.

"You're right," Peggy confirmed. "When we try to offer inclusive activities, the elites often find excuses to be elsewhere. For instance, the last time I invited them to an event, they chose instead to attend an exclusive birthday party for a new resident who had been a bank president. Meanwhile, the newcomers tend to stick together, forming a support network as they deal with their collective history of oppression."

Hannah listened intently, realizing the complexity of her new role. There was much to consider if she was to make a meaningful contribution to the community.

###

Months passed swiftly, and Peggy graciously allowed Hannah to conduct the worship service on the Sunday before Thanksgiving. Initially, Hannah felt intimidated, aware that some of her ancestors had served as domestics in the affluent communities of the North Shore, from where many residents of Rivercrest Center originated. The prospect of ministering to these individuals caused her to hesitate, burdened by unaddressed feelings regarding privilege, racism, and wealth. Hannah was uncertain, feeling like an outsider in an environment with deeply entrenched norms and traditions that she might never fully grasp or understand.

Hannah made her way to the chapel. Her anxiety began to fade as the residents arrived, displaying their diversity. Some approached in wheelchairs and walkers; others used canes or walked unaided into the room, taking their seats with expectancy and reverence. As Hannah observed their entrance into the worship space, it became clear that she and the residents were drawn together for the same reason—they were all spiritual children of God, seeking another opportunity to worship. They had gathered to affirm their faith, united in spirit, expressing their closeness to a transcendent and holy being.

That day, Hannah delivered a sermon entitled "Songs in the Key of G." In it, she recounted a moment when she felt overwhelmed standing in her kitchen and listening to grim news on the radio. But as the broadcast ended, a song began to play, its lyrics lifting her spirits and reminding her that God ultimately has the final say. Hannah expressed her belief that God communicates through the majesty of nature and that music is another medium for interaction. She urged the congregation to express their gratitude and rejoice because God was the force that resolves the symphonies of life.

She shared the story of Thomas A. Dorsey, who experienced a profound spiritual transformation and later a devastating personal tragedy that temporarily halted his music career. Yet, solitude and reflection led him to compose "Precious Lord," now celebrated as one of the greatest gospel songs. Hannah also mentioned Ludwig von Beethoven and Henry Van Dyke, illustrating how personal struggles can translate into expressions of trust, joy, and hope through music. Lastly, she spoke of Horatio Spafford, who penned "It Is Well with My Soul" following a tragic loss, embodying a profound acknowledgment of God's mercy. Throughout her sermon, Hannah communicated that regardless of life's challenges, it was possible to declare, "It is well with my soul," because she had learned to find peace and balance in any situation.

###

After the worship service, Hannah strolled along the river. Its commanding presence enveloped her in a firm embrace. Under Hannah's contemplative gaze, the river transcended its earthly bounds. It became a sacred narrative, a flowing tapestry of life's journey, anointed by God. In sync with the river's powerful undulations, Hannah's heart swelled with profound empathy for all beings adrift on life's tumultuous currents. Just as the Spirit once hovered over the waters to coax order from chaos, the river chanted an anthem of creation and passage, surmounted obstacles, and reached horizons. Gazing toward the horizon where the water kissed the sky, Hannah was moved to spiritual reflections. As the river embraced change, so must we learn to navigate life's transformations, preserving the beauty and vitality of the waters and creating a deeper understanding of our existence, resilience, and timeless bond with God. Amen and Ashe.

18

2030 **Roberta's Battle**

It was family day at Rivercrest. Roberta, who had become a resident at Rivercrest Center, was assigned the role of storyteller to the children visiting the facility. She gathered the children around her, her eyes twinkling with the excitement of sharing a cherished tale.

"Come closer, my dears," she began, her voice soft yet filled with vibrant strength. "Let me tell you the remarkable story of hope, transformation, and a mysterious benefactor whose generosity forever changed the lives of the people of Lewis Town."

"Years ago, long before you could see the bustling shops and hear the laughter from the playgrounds, our town resembled a canvas waiting for a burst of color. The community, including your great-grandparents and their friends, held vast dreams that could fill the sky. They were part of a dedicated Task Force striving to bring about a new dawn for Lewis Town. Despite their hard work, progress came in trickles—a little here, a little there, never quite enough to paint the grand picture they envisioned."

Roberta paused, ensuring the children were captivated. "Our town was resilient yet weary, yearning for a miracle. And, oh, did that miracle arrive! It seemed as though fate itself had heard our pleas. The news that changed everything flowed through our streets like a refreshing spring after a harsh drought."

She leaned in closer, her voice dropping to a whisper as if sharing a sacred secret. "A young woman, once a young girl from our very streets, who ventured far and wide and made a fortune in the bustling world of real estate, never forgot her roots here in the south side of Lewis Town. Upon her passing, a stunning revelation came to light. She left behind a will, bequeathing a staggering part of her billion-dollar fortune to our humble town. And she wished to remain an anonymous shero, a silent guardian angel."

Roberta's hands gestured wildly as she described the transformation. "Imagine, children, waking up to find that the worn paths you walked were lined with vibrant gardens, that the old, tired playgrounds were to be replaced with bright new ones brimming with joy and laughter. Once burdened with the heavy task of finding funds, our city leaders were suddenly the stewards of this incredible gift. Everything changed overnight."

Roberta's voice filled with warmth. "As the town blossomed anew, so did the spirit of its people. Walking through Lewis Town now, you see smiles that shine a little brighter and feel more hopeful, not just because of the new surroundings, but because of a renewed belief in our community's potential."

She looked each young visitor in the eye, her expression earnest. "So, remember, as we walk through our revitalized town, every paved street, every blooming park, speaks of hope and generosity. It tells us that you can always make a difference no matter where life takes you. Our mysterious benefactor didn't just rebuild structures; she rebuilt spirits, teaching us that any community can dream and achieve those dreams with kindness and support."

Her voice was resonant with emotion. Roberta concluded, "And that, my dear children, is how Lewis Town was transformed, bound forever by love, justice, and the joy of a reborn community. Each day, as we enjoy our town's new lease on life, we also honor the spirit of a woman who believed deeply in the power of giving back—a true shero whose legacy will guide us for generations to come." The children, moved and inspired, nestled closer, their young hearts filled with dreams of their own, ready to continue the legacy of their cherished Lewis Town.

###

Ashley, supervisor of the memory care units, was a compassionate and dedicated professional who oversaw the daily operations with a profound understanding of the unique needs of individuals with dementia and Alzheimer's. Her commitment to personalized care and attention was evident in every unit detail. She guided Denise through the corridors, pointing out the rooms designed to resemble a hospital yet softened with wooden nightstands and dressers. These elements and other amenities were thoughtfully placed on fostering a sense of home for the residents. As they moved through the units, Denise observed that many residents were resting, either asleep or quietly reclining. She took note of those who seemed open to a chat later that day.

During their walk, Ashley shared insights on the importance of being attentive and adaptable when engaging with the residents, especially those in the memory care unit. She recounted an event that had deeply impacted her when she first started working there. It was a Sunday morning during a worship service held for residents with dementia. The liturgical team had just finished reading scriptures, praying, and singing hymns. To Ashley's surprise, a resident she assumed was asleep started smiling. This unexpected reaction prompted Ashley to reflect on how even those who seemed disengaged could still connect with spiritual activities, stirring a deeper consideration of how to meet the spiritual needs of individuals with dementia. Spurred by this revelation, Ashley began incorporating more familiar songs, psalms, and prayers into daily activities, choices inspired by their ability to tap into deep-seated memories of the residents. She noticed that even if some residents could not sing the words, they often found comfort and joy in softly reciting them.

Impressed by Ashley's approach, Denise shared her experience, which underscored music's power. She recalled a time in the break room with several residents, where old hymns played over the intercom. The music seemed to trigger a profound response; residents who hadn't spoken in weeks suddenly began recounting memories of the songs. Their stories were rich with details about past events, people, and places, shared within the limits of their current communication abilities. Denise's experience reinforced the belief that music and familiar sounds could awaken deeply embedded, cherished memories, offering the residents moments of joy and connection.

###

Denise revisited the memory care unit occasionally. It was filled with a gentle hum of soft music and the murmur of conversations that created a soothing atmosphere. Walking through the cozy common area, she noticed residents enjoying their meals together, a scene that warmed her heart.

"It's truly inspiring to see how you manage everything with such care," Denise remarked to Ashley as they walked. Ashley smiled, appreciating the acknowledgment of her hard work.

"Thank you, Denise. It's challenging but essential. We focus a lot on creating a supportive and enriching environment here. It's all about enhancing our residents' quality of life," Ashley explained.

Denise listened intently, her eyes opening to the specialized support provided by the unit. The staff, trained specifically in dementia care, employed effective communication strategies and behavioral management to offer compassionate support to the residents.

"I can see that safety and security are top priorities here," Denise observed, noting the carefully crafted environment designed to minimize risks and reduce confusion for the residents.

"Absolutely," Ashley agreed. "We also ensure that each resident receives a personalized care plan tailored to their preferences and needs. It's crucial for supporting their daily activities and respecting their dignity and autonomy."

As they continued, Ashley highlighted the cognitive stimulation activities available—memory games, music therapy, art projects, and reminiscence therapy—all aimed at maintaining cognitive acuity and enhancing social interaction. The opportunities for socialization particularly touched Denise.

"It's wonderful how you foster community and belonging here. I can imagine it does wonders for their mood and helps reduce feelings of isolation," she commented.

"Yes, and it's all part of being in a senior living center with a continuum of care. This setup allows for easy transitions between different services as our residents' needs change, ensuring continuity within the same community," Ashley added.

She also spoke about the services extended to the residents' families, which included educational programs and support groups to help them understand more about dementia and effective caregiving strategies.

"We take extraordinary measures to ensure the safety and comfort of our residents, and we offer specialized activities and therapies to enhance their well-being," Ashley explained as they neared the end of their tour.

Denise said, "Thank you for showing me around, Ashley. Everyone here receives thorough and compassionate care. It's very reassuring to see."

Ashley nodded, pleased to share the inner workings of her passion. "I'm glad you feel that way. It's all about making a difference in their lives daily."

###

As Denise meticulously organized the game closet in the activity lounge at Rivercrest Center, the sound of a gentle knock interrupted the quiet bumping of her work. Turning around, she was greeted by Roberta's familiar, comforting presence. Denise knew Roberta when they lived in Lewis Town and participated in task force planning with Denise's mother, Hannah.

"It's only me," Roberta said softly, easing herself into the room. "I just wanted to drop by and keep you company. I can see you're busy. Don't stop on my account."

Denise couldn't help but smile warmly at her. "No problem at all. I'm always happy to see you," she replied, grateful for the interruption.

Roberta moved towards the big picture window and settled into a chair, her gaze lingering on the trees outside, their leaves dancing whimsically in the wind.

"Everything must change," she mused aloud, her voice a blend of reflection and melancholy. Denise paused her work, drawn into the moment, sensing the depth of the conversation that was about to unfold.

"Watching those leaves," Roberta continued, "it's remarkable, right? How each one embarks on a profound journey through the seasons. It's a cycle of birth, life, decay, and rebirth. Such a visible and invisible transformation that holds deeper meanings, mirroring our own human experiences."

Denise responded. "It's like nature's way of teaching us about renewal and letting go, I believe."

Roberta nodded, her eyes reflecting a pool of lived wisdom. "Exactly. And it teaches us resilience, too. Each season brings its challenges and beauties. Like these leaves, we too have time to grow, shine, and eventually let go, making way for new growth."

The younger woman absorbed these words, finding an unexpected solace in them. "It's comforting, in a way, to think about change like that. Not just as an end, but as a necessary part of a larger, beautiful cycle."

Roberta's gaze returned to Denise, a gentle firmness in her voice.

"My dear, the beauty of getting older is that you see the patterns repeat in nature and life. You learn that endings are not just endings but also beginnings. Each phase of life, with its joys and trials, is crucial. It's all interconnected."

Denise moved closer, sitting beside Roberta, drawn into the tranquility of her perspective. "I think that's a beautiful way to look at life. It makes the tough times seem less permanent, more a part of something endless."

Roberta smiled, her eyes brightening. "That's the spirit. And remember, every day is a chance to renew, to start fresh, even in small ways."

The room was filled with a comfortable silence that wrapped around them like a warm blanket as both women sat, watching the world outside cycle through its natural rhythm. Each leaf's dance was a quiet testament to life's enduring, ever-renewing spirit. Amen and Ashe.

19

2031 **Fall Gives Way To Winter**

Roberta was diagnosed with Alzheimer's disease, an unfortunate event that necessitated her move to the assisted living facility. Hannah made it her duty to visit her old friend weekly. Initially, Roberta engaged actively in their conversations, expressing her presence, desires, and needs. However, as the disease advanced, Roberta's ability to communicate dwindled to non-verbal cues like eye contact and deliberate body movements. Hannah recalled her experiences as a hospital chaplain with patients during these times. She endeavored to bring peace and light into Roberta's life, employing a ministry of presence to ignite hope. Hannah aimed to offer encouragement, friendship, and support, helping to alleviate Roberta's fears about the future. Her visits varied in length, sometimes merely involving a brief check-in to see if Roberta needed anything.

On the days when Roberta was lucid, Hannah began her visits by inquiring about her well-being, to which Roberta often responded that she was "cold and hungry." Taking this as her cue, Hannah fetched an extra blanket from the linen rack and grabbed a snack for Roberta, which usually sufficed for a while. There were also days when Roberta preferred solitude. Upon Hannah's arrival on such days, Roberta would close her eyes and lower her head, feigning sleep. On other occasions, Roberta kept her eyes partially open, and Hannah would sit beside her, recounting recent events, though the conversation was largely one-sided. Despite her inability to actively participate, Roberta gave subtle signs of listening. Hannah knew it was time to leave when Roberta began to fidget in her chair and scowl.

###

During one of Hannah's visits, she observed Roberta sitting alone at the game table. Roberta's skin was marked by deep wrinkles that etched her face. Her eyes, once bright and vibrant, now appeared dull and vacant. She moved slowly and with great effort, as if each movement was a burden. Despite her physical and mental decline, there was still a sense of grace and dignity about her that was evident even in her confused state.

Roberta had been a college professor for many years before her illness took hold, and she possessed a sharp mind and a love for learning. On her nightstand lay a collection of well-worn and beloved books, evidence of a life spent pursuing knowledge. She often spent time in her room, flipping through the pages of her favorite books, her face lighting up with recognition as she read familiar passages. When Roberta was a girl, the library had been a sanctuary. There, the air was filled with the smell of aging ink and decaying paper. The odor of dry rot mingled with the scent of the lemon oil the janitor used to add luster to the thick hardwood tables and countertops.

As a frequent visitor in those days long ago, Roberta knew precisely where to find epic tales about justice, courage, might, and other lofty themes. Occasionally, she settled for a good adventure or a science fiction tale. Roberta especially loved books about places she wanted to go and sights she wanted to behold. Her favorite stories described journeys she wanted to take and spoke of passions she wanted to feel. Because she loved reading so much, Roberta had a way with words. She naturally drew people in with her storytelling. She had a way of painting vivid pictures with her words, creating a captivating narrative that left listeners hanging on every phrase.

Though words escaped Roberta these days, her sweet and gentle nature came through. Despite her moments of confusion and frustration, she remained a beacon of light, a reminder of the resilience of the human spirit. In her quiet way, Roberta touched the hearts of all who knew her, leaving a lasting impression that would never be forgotten.

###

On the day of Hannah's visit, Roberta focused on a crumb of bread left behind after breakfast. She poked and patted at the breadcrumb, oblivious to everything else around her.

"Are you up for a visit, Roberta?" Hannah asked.

Roberta answered her with a blank stare. It was as if some thief had come to her in the middle of the night and robbed her of every single one of her memories. Today, Roberta was not inclined to remember what day it was, where she was, or even what she had for breakfast—if she had eaten.

After she left Roberta that day, Hannah's thoughts centered on how best to interact with her friend, who navigated the foggy paths of dementia. Hannah understood deeply that approaching someone with dementia like Roberta required a foundation of patience, empathy, and a profound respect for their current reality. She noted that a gentle demeanor was essential—soft tones in speech, tender smiles, and maintaining eye contact could make a difference. These simple gestures were not just acts of kindness but crucial signals of safety and familiarity to someone whose sense of the world might be shifting unpredictably.

Communication, Hannah mused, should be stripped down to its essence. She believed in using straightforward, familiar language and avoiding the complexities of abstract thinking that could lead to confusion. Speaking slowly was also crucial, allowing Roberta the necessary time to process the spoken words and respond in her own time, thus preserving her dignity and sense of involvement. Hannah also recognized the power of non-verbal communication. A warm expression, a thoughtful gesture, or a gentle touch—if welcome—could communicate more than words. These non-verbal cues were vital for connecting with Roberta, providing comfort and reinforcing their bond significantly as her verbal abilities waned.

Moreover, Hannah saw the value in engaging Roberta with activities that echoed her past interests. Reminiscing about her days as a professor, discussing beloved books, or sharing cherished memories could significantly boost Roberta's spirits and self-esteem. These conversations were not mere distractions but vital links to her identity and a testament to her life's passions.

As Hannah organized these insights, she envisioned the visitors who would come by, each eager to connect with their loved ones, yet unsure how. Hannah decided to record her insights into a pamphlet, hoping to bridge the gap between uncertainty and meaningful interaction, creating moments of joy and recognition for patients like Roberta and their visitors alike.

###

As Roberta's condition took a turn for the worse, her health declined gradually. Her body lost the capacity to heal, to breathe independently, and, ultimately, to sustain life. She suffered multiple minor strokes that led her into a state resembling a coma. Recent diagnostic tests showed severe damage to an artery critical for supplying oxygen to her brain, indicating a permanent decline in both her physical and cognitive abilities. Roberta became entirely dependent on others for her day-to-day care. The drastic reduction in her quality of life brought her interdisciplinary care team and loved ones to the heart-wrenching decision to cease life-sustaining support.

On the designated Friday, Hannah remained by Roberta's bedside during the last hours of her shift, maintaining a solemn vigil. She filled Roberta's final moments with prayers and passages from scripture, providing comfort in the quiet hospital room. Roberta passed away in the early hours of a windy Saturday. Although grieving the loss, Hannah felt peace knowing that her friend had found sanctuary in a realm beyond her earthly concerns.

###

In the aftermath of her close friend Roberta's death, Hannah sought comfort by the river, a place where nature's serenity seemed to soothe her aching heart. As she walked along the riverfront, it felt like Roberta's spirit was right there with her, sharing in the quiet moments of reflection. The gentle currents of the river whispered, providing a calming backdrop to Hannah's introspective journey. Sunlight poured over the landscape, casting long, comforting shadows that seemed to dance gently around her. In this tranquil setting, Hannah found the space to reminisce and feel connected to the memories of her dear friend.

Hannah detoured through the cemetery, drawn closer to where her friend would rest. Surrounded by a sea of graves and tombstones, she was struck by the silent stories each one held—lives once vibrant, now remembered with carefully crafted headstones that spoke of deep reverence and respect. Wandering through the orderly rows, Hannah's attention was captured by a unique headstone that stood out from the others. It was modest yet striking, marked only with "Mother Epiphany, An Ancestor." The absence of a surname or dates left its history shrouded in mystery. Yet, it seemed to whisper secrets of a bygone era directly to Hannah, sparking a deep curiosity within her. Perhaps it was more than chance that led her to this grave; perhaps it was the guiding hand of Ashe—the spiritual force believed to imbue the universe with potentialities of existence in the Yoruba tradition. Many formidable souls had navigated the tumultuous waters of their lives with nothing but the grace of God, the blood of Jesus, the power of the Holy Spirit, and the force of Ashe—all of which balance the equations of life and make change happen. This force seemed to resonate in the air, infusing the space with a spirit of indomitability.

Hannah had thought of her ancestors that morning as a warm breeze perfumed with Nadia wafted through her screened-in porch. Now, standing before Mother Epiphany's grave, Hannah felt a deep connection to her lineage. She contemplated the legacy she wanted to craft, inspired by the resilience and strength of those before her. The silent testimonies of the surrounding headstones, each a monument to a life once lived, echoed within her, urging her to grasp her own life's meaning. In the moment of quiet reflection, Hannah realized her purpose was intertwined with the legacies of these ancestors. Every decision and action she took was a continuation of their stories, adding to the ongoing narrative of her family. Empowered by the spirit of the ancestors, just as Mother Epiphany and countless others were, she felt ready to rise above her challenges. Hannah envisioned her legacy as more than a simple inscription on a headstone; she wanted it to be impactful and meaningful and to touch the lives of others, bringing peace, enlightenment, and understanding. Her story would inspire, uplift, and serve as a beacon of hope and resilience for future generations.

With renewed determination, Hannah left the cemetery, the headstone image etched in her mind. She carried not only the stories of her past but also the unbreakable spirit of her ancestors, prepared to face the future with courage and a soul ignited by her ancestors' indomitable wills. Surrounded by the silent witnesses of the cemetery, Hannah had felt a profound sense of purpose. She was determined to ensure that her experiences and the wisdom she gained would resonate long after she was gone, serving a purpose greater than herself. She silently vowed to strive for a legacy rooted in compassion, empathy, and the pursuit of peace and understanding. As Hannah resumed her walk along the river, the rhythmic flow of the water echoed her renewed sense of purpose. With each step, she committed to leaving a legacy that would endure, inspire, and illuminate the lives of those yet to come.

###

The weight of her responsibilities as the officiant settled heavily on Hannah's shoulders. The solemn service was an intimate gathering of friends and loved ones now assembled under a small tent, where chairs in short rows offered a space of shared mourning. The gentle rustling of leaves and the murmur of the gathered friends and family seemed to pause as Hannah began the ceremony. The profound unity of her opening remarks drew together the threads of many individual sorrows into a tapestry of shared remembrance. Today, her voice set a respectful and reflective tone, inviting each person present to contemplate the significance of the gathering.

As the service unfolded, the air filled with the resonance of prayers and readings that held a deep significance for Roberta and her loved ones. Hannah had spent hours selecting these texts—some drawn from religious traditions, others from beloved poems or favorite passages, each chosen to comfort and guide those gathered in their grief. She knew the power of these words to speak to hearts wracked by loss, offering a balm to the soul in moments of profound sorrow.

The eulogy, delivered by a close family member, wove together laughter and tears—a mosaic of memories that painted a vivid portrait of Roberta's life. Hannah listened, her heart full, as anecdotes and accolades spilled forth, each underscoring Roberta's indelible impact on those around her. These stories, these shared moments, truly celebrated Roberta's journey through life, her achievements, her joys, and even her challenges.

When the time came for the committal, the atmosphere turned solemn. The final blessings were spoken, and the rituals of farewell—a gentle lowering of the casket, the symbolic placement of earth upon it—marked this poignant transition. Hannah felt every eye upon her as she officiated this final act, a profound goodbye that seemed to acknowledge both the finality of death and the eternal memory of life. As the ceremony concluded, participants came forward to lay flowers upon the grave. Hannah found this act particularly moving; each bloom was a silent testament to love, memory, and respect. It was a simple gesture, yet it transformed the site into a place of beauty and peace. Hannah's final words as officiant brought comfort and closure, allowing everyone a moment to reflect, mourn, and heal. The words lingered in the crisp air, a gentle benediction over the assembled mourners.

Later, at the reception, as stories and condolences were exchanged over a shared meal, Hannah observed the subtle shift from mourning to remembrance. In this space of fellowship, it was here that the community indeed came together to honor Roberta's memory—a celebration of a life well-lived, echoing in the laughter and tears of those she had left behind. For Hannah, each funeral was a profound reminder of life's fragility and the strength of human connections. Today, as ever, she felt honored to lead such a ceremony, embracing the blend of cultural, religious, and personal rituals that beautifully reflected the lives and the legacies of people who have reached their eternal destination.

###

A comforting touch seemed to rest on Hannah in the solemn stillness following the burial, enveloping her in an embrace as comforting as the cloudless sky. Bearing the heavy cloak of cumulative grief, she found herself at a vulnerable crossroads, where the temptation to succumb to emotional weariness was ever-present. Hannah's life journey had been marked by profound loss and a deep connection to the infinite line of her ancestors, whose spirits intertwined with the very essence of existence. She felt the enduring power of the vital spiritual force that courses through all beings, binding her to the past and future generations. This ancient strength whispered of resilience and continuity, urging her to navigate the tumultuous waters ahead for the sake of those who would one day follow in her wake.

Through her grief, Hannah found unique ways to honor her departed loved ones. She integrated their memories into the daily tapestry of her life, allowing their spirits to live on vibrantly in her actions and thoughts. Each memory stitched with love into her days helped fortify her against the waves of sorrow. Holding onto hope, even during those bleakest moments, she was guided by a luminescent trail of wisdom and inner peace. The light did not merely illuminate her path but also guided her towards healing and understanding, enabling her to manage her peace amidst the storms of emotion. Hannah carried the sacred echo of "Amen and Ashe" in her heart, respectfully acknowledging her spiritual journey and the unbreakable bond with her ancestry. This connection to eternity and ancestral power became her beacon, motivating her to persevere for herself and all the generations that would follow. Each step forward was a testament to the undying force of life and continuity. Amen and Ashe.

Epilogue: 2051

As Hannah and Phillip settled into their quaint cottage at the Rivercrest Senior Living Center, they embarked on an exhilarating new adventure. Phillip and Hannah had recently transitioned to their charming new home, marking a fresh life chapter. Although smaller, their new residence offered a cozy and adequate living space. Nestled by the gentle river, their new home was a beacon of comfort, equipped with every modern convenience they desired. This delightful home provided a peaceful retreat filled with modern amenities and was surrounded by meticulously tended gardens, eliminating the need for lawn care and maintenance.

This idyllic environment was a stark departure from Hannah's early years in the economically challenged southern districts of Lewis Town, which were deeply affected by urban renewal efforts that fragmented her community and altered the landscape of her childhood. Reflecting on her journey, Hannah often thought about her ancestors' sacrifices. They had traversed formidable barriers so that she could have a better life. Now, residing in the elegance and security of Rivercrest, she felt a deep connection to those past struggles, realizing how they had woven the fabric of her present comfort and peace. The poetic justice of returning to a community that once displaced her family was not lost on Hannah. This twist of fate had brought her a profound sense of closure and renewal. At Rivercrest, she had rediscovered a sense of belonging, finding camaraderie and friendship in faces that once seemed foreign. This experience underscored a profound truth: despite life's tumultuous waves, all were bound by a common humanity, journeying through life's phases together.

Together, Phillip and Hannah embraced the vibrant life Rivercrest offered. They had become regulars at the health club, their laughter echoing in the gym, and they had enjoyed many meals in the center's charming restaurants, each dish a delightful surprise crafted by expert chefs. The couple cherished the impeccably maintained gardens, where they took strolls, relishing the meticulous care that went into every shrub and pathway.

They had sincerely hoped to spend their remaining years in this haven of tranquility, surrounded by natural beauty and the warm company of old and new friends. God willing, they wished to continue this chapter of their lives, where every day brought new joys and the promise of care and dignity in their twilight years. This was more than a new residence for Hannah and Phillip—it had fulfilled dreams, a testament to a life's journey marked by resilience and the pursuit of happiness.

###

The Rivercrest Grand Ballroom had been transformed into a dazzling display of elegance and festivity for Hannah and Phillip's wedding anniversary. The room was adorned with twinkling lights, beautiful flowers, and photos depicting their long and happy life together. Denise, her husband Mark, and their kids, Iris and David, attended the festivities to share the joy of the occasion, along with many friends, family, and fellow residents of the community.

The room where Hannah and Phillip made their grand entrance was bathed in a warm, inviting glow. The soft strains of their favorite melodies filled the air, played by a live band whose tunes seemed to weave seamlessly into the fabric of the evening. Subtle lighting cast a gentle luminescence, highlighting arrangements of delicate flowers whose fragrances mingled with the scent of aged wood and polished silver, creating an atmosphere of refined celebration.

Though his hair had silvered and his posture curved with the years, Phillip still carried an air of dignified presence. His suit, impeccably tailored, added to his venerable stature. Beside him, equally graceful Hannah wore her advanced years with an understated elegance. Time had touched her features softly, bringing a wise and understanding gaze, yet she retained the vibrant allure that had first captured Phillip's heart.

The couple stepped onto the dance floor as the band struck an exceptionally sentimental tune. The years seemed to fall away as they moved together in a dance of quiet synchrony, their movements slower now but every bit as full of affection and deep connection. Each step and gentle sway was a testament to their enduring love, a dance of memories and shared dreams. Even as their bodies spoke of age, their spirits danced with the timeless rhythm of life-long partners, deeply in tune and eternally devoted.

Throughout the evening, guests took turns sharing heartfelt stories and memories, recounting funny anecdotes and touching moments from Hannah and Phillip's many decades together. Laughter filled the room as guests reconnected and new friendships were formed. When it was their time for remarks, Denise and Mark walked hand in hand to the podium, beaming with excitement.

"Happy Anniversary, Mom and Dad! We are very proud of you." Mark, a man of few words, shared how Phillip had been a fantastic role model, working hard his whole life to achieve his goals. "We love you." Mark expressed.

Denise stepped up to the podium alongside Mark.

"Mom and Dad, I share Mark's sentiments wholeheartedly. Mom, I am particularly grateful to have you as my guide. You began your journey under modest circumstances, yet you faced every obstacle with courage. You consistently aimed to uplift and empower others, even when it meant putting your needs aside. I remember the sacrifices you made of your time, talents, and treasures during the fight for justice and change. We stood at the crossroads and protested injustice. That's where we lost Calvin in the fight for freedom. Yet, you continued to dedicate your soul to advancing the cause. You poured your peace and light into the lives of people you cared for. And now those efforts have shown results. You were an excellent role model.

"Every day, I strive to follow the example you set. There was no challenge too great for you, buoyed as you were by an unwavering faith in God that ensured you never found yourself sinking. Thank you for your wisdom and resilience. Thank you for your relentless pursuit of truth and justice. I love you. I pray that the rest of your journey is filled with blessings and happiness. Congratulations on your wedding anniversary. May God bless you with many more," Denise said with a warm smile.

Hannah felt slightly fragile as Denise came over and hugged her with full strength. Other family members, friends, and colleagues offered kind words, acknowledging Hannah and Phillip as valued community members in a place that was once off-limits to people like them. God is good, they noted.

As the night drew to a close, Hannah and Phillip were presented with a beautiful cake adorned with their names in shimmering gold icing. Everyone gathered around to watch them blow out the candles with difficulty, making a wish for many more years of happiness together.

Guests continued to offer congratulations and heartfelt wishes: "Phillip and Hannah, congratulations on your anniversary! What a beautiful milestone to celebrate here at Rivercrest. Your journey together is truly inspiring, and it's heartwarming to see the love and devotion you share. Here's to many more years of happiness and love!"

The celebration ended with a final dance as Phillip whispered in Hannah's ear. "Hannah, do you remember when we first met all those years ago?" Phillip inquired.

"Of course I do. It feels like just yesterday, doesn't it?" Hannah replied. "And look at us now with all these years of marriage under our belts. We've been through so much together."

"We have, haven't we? But our love has only grown stronger through it all," Phillip remarked.

"That's the beauty of it. No matter our trials, we always had each other to lean on," Hannah added. "I couldn't imagine going through life without you by my side, Phillip. You've been my rock through it all."

"And you've been my guiding light, Hannah. I don't know where I'd be without you," Phillip responded.

"I'm so grateful for every moment we've shared, the good and the bad. The heartbreak and the joy. It's been a journey, but I have no regrets," Hannah said.

"Me neither. Here's to us, my love. Here's to many more years of love and devotion," Phillip concluded, kissing her and hugging her more tightly.

###

Still invigorated by the festivity the day after the party, Hannah and Phillip strolled to the deli, craving an ice cream sundae made with Neapolitan ice cream, generously topped with extra nuts, whipped cream, and cherries. With measured steps to maintain their balance, they navigated the walkway leading to the river, where they eventually sat side by side on Calvin's memorial bench by the riverfront. It was springtime, and the tranquil moment allowed them to reflect on the journey that had brought them to this point.

Hannah reminisced about the tapestry of their shared life, touching upon the trials they had overcome, the death of their son, the joyous moments they had celebrated together, and the enduring love that had been the cornerstone of their relationship. The river was quiet and serene as they watched its ceaseless flow. At that moment, Hannah understood that, regardless of what tomorrow might bring, God had accompanied them on every step of their journey, helping them to remain upright and face every trial and joy. A blanket of gratitude enveloped Hannah in a profound peace.

As dusk fell, Hannah and Phillip turned their gaze towards the sky, admiring the beauty of the distant shore as the sun slowly dipped below the horizon. Amen and Ashe.

www.ingramcontent.com/pod-product-compliance
Lightning Source LLC
Chambersburg PA
CBHW070627310726
48982CB00001B/196

* 9 7 9 8 3 8 5 2 2 4 8 1 4 *